Reviews:

*"Amanda Lauer brings history to life in this fast-paced, emotionally charged, splendid tale. Extremely enjoyable."*
May McGoldrick, International Bestselling Author of *The Thistle and Rose, Secret Vows* and *the Highland Treasure Trilogy*

*"The South of 1864 springs to life in 'A World Such as Heaven Intended.' Rich in details of language, setting and social mores, Lauer takes readers on the journey of her protagonist, Amara McKirnan, a strong woman ahead of her time who wrestles with her blended family and the horrors of the Civil War to find the peace and happiness she is convinced awaits her."*
Marni Graff, Author, *The Nora Tierney Mysteries*

*"'A World Such as Heaven Intended' is a fast-moving historical romance which will keep you turning pages until the very end! An excellent read."*
Patrice Fagnant-MacArthur, Author, *The Catholic Baby Name Book*

*"A charming romance with well-drawn characters and clear imagery, offering the reader a chance to slip away to another era and come home refreshed."*
A.K. Frailey, Author, *The Deliverance Trilogy*

A World
Such As Heaven Intended

A Civil War Romance

By Amanda Lauer

FQ Publishing
Pakenham, Ontario

A World Such as Heaven Intended
copyright 2014
by Amanda Lauer

Published by Full Quiver Publishing
PO Box 244
Pakenham, Ontario K0A 2X0

ISBN Number: 978-0-9879153-6-8
Printed and bound in the USA

Cover photos: Anna Coltran of Belle Gente Photography
Cover design: James Hrkach

NATIONAL LIBRARY OF CANADA
CATALOGUING IN PUBLICATION

Copyright 2014 by Amanda Lauer
Published by Full Quiver Publishing
A Division of Innate Productions

*To John*
*my first, my last, my everything*

# Chapter I

She was ill-prepared for the sight her eyes beheld as she stood in the entryway to the sizeable room. Cots filled nearly every square inch of the space that had once been a grand ballroom. Scanning the area from end to end, the surreal fog she had been living in for the last three years was whisked away like a sheer curtain being torn from a window. The godforsaken men lying upon makeshift beds became very real to her—no longer just souls spoken of discreetly behind fans held in the fingertips of Atlanta's ladies of good quality.

Amara had been in this room many times before but under far different circumstances. She could recall an incident from her childhood where she stood on this very same spot. After tiptoeing up the curved stairs to the entryway, she had peeked around one of the massive double doors to observe countless duos sweeping across the gleaming wooden floor in perfect synchrony. As the small orchestra performed a waltz, one couple in particular stood out. The stately gentleman covered the space agilely, an enchanting woman in his arms. She was cloaked in a beautiful aqua gown that flattered her slender figure. The two were entranced in each other's gaze, oblivious to their daughter's loving perusal.

That was one of many fond memories tucked deep away in Amara's mind. Fresher, much less pleasant snippets filled her head to the point where Amara began to wonder if the good days had ever actually existed. As if on command, the recent recollection of her mother came to her—watching her fade away over the course of several months as the consumption drew the life out of her. Although it had been four years ago, the sense of helplessness and despair felt so real that it could have happened yesterday. Shaking her head, Amara refocused on the scene in front of her and realized what she witnessed in her mother's last days paled in comparison to the view before her at this moment.

"They're the fortunate ones," said the orderly, after clearing his throat to get Amara's attention. "These fellas are the ones who stand a chance of survival and, if it's the will of God," the man paused to swipe the cap off his head and hold it over his heart, "they'll live to rejoin their Confederate units. The fate of the soldiers in the rooms below, I won't lie to you, Miss, it's grim. I can show you around down there when you have a few minutes."

Amara shook her head. There was only so much she could handle at once. She was already doing her best to quell the urge to pick up her skirts and scamper back down the stairs and out the front door she had just stepped through minutes before. *What in the world have I gotten myself into?*

"No, thank you, sir. But I appreciate your kind offer. I'm sure I'll see everything in due time."

The orderly repositioned his cap and proceeded into the room. Amara stepped in behind him, keeping close to his heels. She tried to keep her eyes focused past his shoulder to the crucifix hung on the far wall but she couldn't stop herself from glancing around the room as they made their way across the space. *Hail Mary, full of grace...* A number of men were wrapped in blood-soaked bandages. *The Lord is with thee...* Some had head wounds and several had broken bones set in splints. *Blessed art thou amongst women...* The bile rose in her throat at the ghastly display of raw stumps from missing limbs. *And blessed is the fruit of thy womb, Jesus...* If the sight of the injuries wasn't bad enough, the stench in the room was unbearable. *Holy Mary, mother of God, pray for us sinners...* Amara pulled the lavender-scented handkerchief from her sleeve and held it over her nose. The odor engulfing the room gagged her, yet her guide didn't seem to notice it. *Now and at the hour of our death. Amen.*

Having spent many an idle day as a child helping her Uncle William in his physician's office in the lower level of the building, Amara thought aiding him at the infirmary would be a simple enough task. But cutting and folding bandages and straightening shelves of medicinal cures had not prepared her for this ghoulish encounter.

The orderly paused to glance back at Amara and a look of concern crossed his face. Just then a low moaning sound came from a man lying on a cot near where they stood. The orderly stepped closer and gently pulled back the sheet covering the man's upper half. His arm was heavily bruised and the upper bone had a peculiar angle to it.

Amara's eyes widened upon the sight and she could feel the color creeping up her face, whether it was red or green, she couldn't say.

"We'll get that bone set as soon as your number's called, soldier," reassured the orderly. The man gave a slight nod in acknowledgement, biting his lip to muffle the sounds threatening to escape from his throat again.

Amara couldn't pull her eyes away from the macabre scene. She slowly backed away from the injured soldier and nearly jumped out of her skin when a hand locked onto her elbow and turned her around. Recognizing the man behind the owlish spectacles, Amara's knees nearly buckled in relief.

"Uncle William!"

The man loosened his grip on her and gave her a weary

smile, but refrained from the embrace which was his normal greeting for his only niece. Amara thought it was slightly odd until she glanced down at his blood-splattered shirt.

"Amara, darlin'," said the older man. "So good to see you."

Amara jerked her head up. "And you as well, sir," she stammered.

With a nod of his head, and a quick thank you, the doctor sent the orderly downstairs to retrieve a stretcher. He then turned his full attention to Amara. "You're looking well, my dear," he said, scanning her from head to toe. "A bit on the lean side, but that's to be expected in these times."

"You appear well yourself, Uncle William," she replied automatically, focusing on his face and not the crimson-stained attire. In reality, he looked to be a man ten years older than the William Burgess she saw a mere five months before. He was a stocky man and, while always a bit on the shorter side, he seemed to have lost an inch or two in height as his shoulders were hunched forward—most likely from bending over patients day in and day out, Amara surmised. His mutton chop beard was now sprinkled with gray and the scowl lines on his forehead were more pronounced.

Becoming conscious of her scrutiny, the doctor glanced down at his shirt and unrolled his sleeves to make himself more presentable. "Sorry about that, Amara. It slipped my mind that you'd be here this morning." Tucking a loose shirt end into the top of his trousers, he looked at her over the top of his spectacles. "Not quite what you had in mind when you offered your assistance, eh?"

Shaking her head, Amara replied, "I am not sure if anything could prepare a person for this, to be honest with you, sir." Taking a deep breath, she squared her shoulders and looked the kindly gentleman straight in the eye.

"Uncle William, I do not know what help I can offer, but rest assured, I do plan to hold true to my word and assist you to the best of my ability. Father has fewer customers in his store each day and I cannot tolerate biding my time doing busywork when I know you are in dire need of support here."

"Fair enough," he said, absentmindedly stroking his sideburns with one hand as he assessed his niece with a renewed sense of admiration. He then crossed his arms in front of himself and addressed her in an admonishing tone. "However, young lady, if you intend to put yourself under my charge, you need to dispense with the formalities. Doc is the common moniker for all the physicians on the frontlines. If you call me William, the staff will not know to whom you are referring."

"Yes, sir," said Amara.

"Amara..."

"I mean Doc, sir, um, Doc," she added, garnering his approval.

Continuing on, the man nodded to two similarly dressed, plain-looking women tending to patients on the other side of the room. "As you can see, we have mature females here offering skilled nursing care for the men. What we could use from you is a show of compassion for the soldiers. Offer an encouraging word, read a few verses from the Bible, write letters home to their loved ones..." His voice trailed off as he looked for some form of acknowledgement from his niece.

"I can do that," offered Amara, nodding her head with a sense of relief.

"Very well, then. In that top drawer over there you will find stationery, writing apparatus and a Bible," he said, pointing to the wash stand in the corner of the room. "Thank you again for your assistance," said Doc. "Say hello to your family for me. Lord knows when I'll have free time to stop and pay them a formal visit again." He picked up a sheaf of paper from the foot of an empty bed. "I must continue my rounds. If you have any questions, you may ask the other women in the ward." With a quick bow he was off, leaving Amara to her own devices.

Gingerly making her way between the uneven rows of beds, Amara got to the stand and gathered the supplies she needed. Looking around, she determined her course of action. *I will begin on this end of the room and make my way around to the men who are awake and coherent.*

She timidly approached the nearest cot where a soldier, who appeared not much older than her seventeen years, lay still, his face turned towards the wall.

"Sir, may I be of any assistance to you?"

The young man turned his head in Amara's direction. She was startled to see his eyes completely covered with bandages. "Miss, I can't see you, but you have the voice of an angel. Am I dead or alive?"

"You're quite alive as far as I can tell," said Amara, doing her best to sound cheery.

"Dang. For a second there I thought I actually fooled Saint Peter and made it to the Pearly Gates," said the man dejectedly. "If I'm alive, I guess it means I really can't see. I was hopin' this was all a bad dream and I was gonna wake up starin' at my bunk mate's ugly puss. Of course, that's kind of a nightmare in itself," he said with a chuckle.

Amara admired his sense of humor, considering his circumstances. She smiled as she addressed him. "May I ask your name?"

"My given name is Bartholomew, but my pals call me Bubba."

"Then Bubba it is," said Amara. "My name is Amara McKirnan. I've come to volunteer here at the hospital."

"Hospital?" asked Bubba. "Hmm, what do ya know? Last I remember I was holed up outside Pumpkin Vine

Creek. Saw some Yankees making their way through the woods. Had one of 'em in my sights and went to take a shot and wham, I'm flat on my back and my eyes felt like they was on fire. Next things I knows, I'm here. Where exactly is we?"

"Atlanta. This is my uncle's house. It's been converted to a Confederate hospital like most of the other residences on Capital Square."

"Atlanta?" said Bubba incredulously. "I always heard tell that is one fine city. Hoped to be marchin' into it one of these days ahead of Lee's army. With the ways thing's going nowadays, don't look like me or Lee's going to be seeing the city anytime soon."

"Let's not talk about matters like that right now, shall we," said Amara, hoping to change the track of their conversation. "How about I pen a letter back home to your mama? I'm sure she's concerned about you."

"She ain't much on readin'," he confessed. "But maybe one of the neighbors will come help her decipher it. I know she's been worryin' up a storm about me. Ma's been runnin' the farm since Pa died and me and my brother took off to do us some fightin'. Thought I'd come back a hero and take care of her once we got them Yankees whipped." A sigh escaped before he continued. "Looks like I'm going to be more of a burden to her than a help to her when I do finally get back."

"We'll just write and tell her you've made it through alive," said Amara with conviction.

From there Amara made her way counterclockwise about the space. A number of the patients were in no condition to converse, so she bypassed their cots. Several of the men she met were anxious to send correspondence back home, a few longed to hear a particular Bible passage, and some just wanted to hear a reassuring voice telling them everything would be all right. Amara wasn't necessarily certain things would turn out for all of these soldiers, but she kept a positive demeanor throughout the course of the day and comforted the soldiers in whatever fashion she could.

As Amara approached the final bed, she felt weary from her duties. Her shoulders ached from leaning over the numerous cots, she was perspiring from the oppressive heat, and her head was starting to pound. She appraised the last gentleman as he lay staring up at the ceiling. His eyes appeared to be undamaged. All appendages seemed to be in place. A bandage was wrapped tightly around his bare upper chest, and with the knowledge Amara had picked up over the previous several hours, she assumed he had been injured by grape shot—the cluster of small iron balls discharged from a cannon. The fingers of the man's right hand were firmly clasped on a gold chain suspended around his neck.

"Sir," asked Amara as she stepped closer to the bed, "would you like some company for a few minutes?"

The soldier hastily adjusted the chain, tucked something behind his neck and then put his arm down by his side. He gave Amara a brief glance and then looked away.

Amara cocked her head, waiting for a reply. After a few moments the soldier broke the uncomfortable silence. "No thank you, Miss. I'd just as soon keep company with myself."

She was somewhat taken aback. *That's an odd reply,* Amara mused. Most of the soldiers seemed eager for her companionship. Several of the men had commented that she was a sight for sore eyes. Of course she knew it was just an expression, because in her mind, she was still that gangly, thin-as-a-rail teen sporting a mop of uncontrollable auburn hair. What could any man see in that? Unconsciously she tucked a stray curl behind her ear, something she was wont to do when in a discomfiting situation.

Grabbing her skirt to keep her hand from tucking the hair behind her other ear, Amara did a quick once-over of the man, evaluating him from stem to stern. Even lying down, she could see he was taller than most of the gentlemen of her acquaintance. His black hair had a wave to it and, with his angular facial features and muscular build, he made for one handsome figure. He was a looker, all right. But from experience, Amara knew that the men who cut the most handsome figures were invariably the ones with the largest egos.

She wasn't going to let him get the best of her. Determined to garner a more positive response, Amara put forth a suggestion. "I could write a letter for you. Surely you must have a sweetheart back home who is anxious about your welfare?"

"I assure you, I have no sweetheart pining away for me," said the man bluntly.

Pursing her lips, Amara looked at him closer. The gray standard-issue uniform trousers confirmed he was a Confederate soldier. But he certainly didn't have the Southern drawl she was accustomed to hearing. His arrogance signaled the fact that he was an educated man— she'd met his type before. Her curiosity got the better of her and she pressed on.

"May I inquire where you hail from, Mr. ..." prodded Amara.

"That's Corporal, Miss. Corporal Nathan Michael Edward Simmons, Northern Territory of Texas."

*Texas?* That could certainly clarify a lot of things. While officially it had been a Southern state for nearly twenty years, Amara had heard there were still savages populating the land. *That explains the unfamiliar accent and his questionable manners, but how did he come to be educated? Did they even have schools in that untamed land?*

Looking to wrap up the encounter, Amara made one last inquiry. "Is there anything I *can* do for you, *Corporal* Simmons?"

"I thank you for your offer, but you may go back to your duties of socializing with the other soldiers," said the Texan curtly. "I am sure there are plenty of men who would be happy to make your acquaintance. As for myself, I am perfectly fine on my own."

The blood rushed to Amara's cheeks. It took a moment to muster a fitting reply since the first thing that came to the tip of her tongue was a remark regarding his questionable upbringing.

"As you wish," she responded evenly, turning on her heel. *I have half a mind to pen a letter to his mama myself.* A look of satisfaction came to Amara's face as she pictured an indignant Southern woman marching into the ward and dragging her miserable son off by the ear, wounds be damned.

Chin held high, Amara made her way back to the washstand to return the Bible and writing implements before exiting the room. As she passed the other men, she graciously offered her best wishes and a promise to return the next day. Without a backwards glance, she passed through the doorway, silently closing the elegantly carved doors on her way out. She paused at the top of the steps to consider the perplexing encounter she had with the corporal. Always one to give a person the benefit of the doubt, a thought came to her. *Perhaps he suffered a blow to the skull and he's acting contrary to his usual behavior. That's it!* With a new-found energy, she set off to find Uncle William to tell him that a certain corporal on the second floor needed a thorough examination of his head immediately.

# Chapter II

Amara passed her suggestion along to her uncle, who was holed up in his office. She then headed for the front entrance of the house, keeping her eyes turned away from the parlor which had been converted to a ward for the critically wounded. She had seen enough blood for one day.

Beyond the threshold, her brother James idly lounged against one of the porch columns. It gave Amara a start to see him, crutches under his arms, the empty trouser leg dangling freely. *Maybe it's fate that I'm here at this hospital helping other men who have suffered as much as James has.* Assuming a neutral countenance, she stepped out of the building to greet her brother.

"Hello, Sis. I see you made it through your first day," said James affably.

"That I have, though I wish I could say the same for all of the men in there. That must have been a fearful battle they were waging in Paulding County," replied Amara. "They say General Johnson mauled Hooker's corps but we certainly had our share of casualties."

As James slowly descended the steps, Amara kept close to his side. She wanted to be within arms' reach if he stumbled, but she also wanted to surreptitiously evaluate his condition.

Amara was never quite sure what state she'd find James in at this time of day. He appeared neatly attired, his words weren't slurred and he met her at the given hour—all good signs. But ever since he was shipped home from the army hospital in South Carolina, James hadn't been himself. He suffered from what Uncle William called phantom pain—his leg was gone but the haunting ache still remained. He always kept a bottle of what he referred to as the remedy close at hand. Amara didn't know what the vial contained but, if she had to put money on it, she'd say laudanum. But where he obtained it was beyond her—the tincture was in high demand on the battlefront and in the hospitals. Supplies were getting more difficult to obtain as Yankee ships blockaded more ports along the Southern coastline.

Whatever the remedy was, it seemed to turn James into a different person—a man wandering about in a mist looking for escape from his physical and mental pain. He was certainly not the person she remembered before he set off for war. That boy had been fun-loving and full of life. He could tease her to the point of madness but turned into the protective big brother when the need arose. Those nights when her troubled thoughts left her tossing and turning, he would strum his guitar by her bedside until she drifted off to sleep.

Thankfully, James was coherent and showed an interest in hearing about her day, so Amara elaborated about the past several hours. She chatted as they made their way from Court House Square to their own neighborhood, focusing on her rewarding interactions with the soldiers and skimming over the particulars she wasn't eager to relive, including her encounter with the stranger from Texas.

*Perhaps James has turned a corner*, thought Amara as they made their way past rows of houses and businesses. *Maybe he can deal with his pain without the ever-present bottle.*

As they approached their street, James grabbed her sleeve. "Stop for a minute, will you, Sis? I need just a wee nip before we get home," he said, as he pulled the container from the breast pocket of his gray overcoat.

"Father may be inclined to down a bit of the good grain himself; however, he doesn't approve of me imbibing the remedy. He's under the impression that it's addicting, but I only use it when I can't tolerate the pain anymore," he said emphatically as the bottle was brought to his lips. "Walking these few blocks with you has worn me thin. I need all the strength I can gather to face that malevolent stepmother of ours." With that, he tipped the container back and dribbled a few drops into his mouth. He winced when the liquid hit its mark.

"James," said Amara in a reproachful manner. "Mind what you say!" Neither she nor her brother had an amicable relationship with Mrs. McKirnan. While the woman could see no wrong in her own child, she could see no right in her husband's offspring. Amara theorized that the woman either resented having the added burden of caring for more children or felt they were a threat to the relationship with her husband. Whatever the reason, Amara did her best to keep peace in the family. "You know it's disrespectful to speak ill of our elders. If Father O'Reilly heard you now, he'd have you in the confessional so fast your head would spin."

"Elders," said James with a snort. "That woman isn't more than a handful of years older than Michael. She was probably still in the nursery when Mother and Father married. Youth has served her well though. She was able to snare Father within months of Mother's passing."

A look of horror covered Amara's face. "Are you looking to get smote by the hand of God?" she asked, sending an anxious glance heavenward. "Enough of this subject or I'll be reporting your misdeeds to Father O'Reilly myself."

James relented and the two walked the last block in silence. Before they entered their yard, Amara felt the need to address one concern with her brother. "You don't have to escort me to and from Uncle William's. I've been wearing a path between our two houses for more years than I can remember. I know the way so well I could walk there in my sleep."

"That was before this war started," said James, stopping to address her directly. "You're a young lady now. It is not acceptable, nor safe for that matter, to be walking these streets unescorted."

"Bah! Who's going to bother with me?"

"Have you looked in a mirror lately? You're not the ugly duckling you once were," James said, trying to keep a straight face. He tucked both crutches under one arm and tilted her chin back with his free hand. Surveying first one side of her face then the other, he nodded in approval.

"I've got better things to do than admire myself in the looking glass day in and day out," said Amara, slapping his hand away. "I can still recall my days at the Lucy Cobb Institute witnessing The Lucies obsessing over their looks. I may have only been fourteen when I left there, but I could see that my classmates had more feathers stuffed in their heads than they had perched on top of their fashionable bonnets. But that's neither here nor there. We're home now. Do your best to behave."

"Yes, Ma'am," said James with a mocking bow.

Approaching the dry goods store and their house, Amara intended to stop in and see her father to inquire about the day's business. But the shade was drawn so she knew the shop was closed for the day.

Bracing herself, Amara stepped up to the adjacent doorway and opened the door that led to the McKirnan parlor.

"We're here."

"It's about time," came an irritable voice from the back of the house.

Pasting a smile on her face, Amara made her way to the dining room. "Hello, Mrs. McKirnan. So good to see you. I trust you've had a nice day."

"A nice day? Only if your idea of a nice day is slaving over a hot stove for a stepdaughter who chooses to shirk her household duties so she can save the world, and for a stepson who cannot figure out a way to make himself useful while he lives under our roof. If it weren't for your father and my Theresa, I would have a mind to let you two fend for yourselves and come up with your own meal."

"Mrs. McKirnan, we are grateful for your efforts," said Amara in a conciliatory tone. *Well, at least I'm being truthful about that.* She headed into the kitchen to wash her hands in the basin. *Cooking is one duty I can do without.* She would never consider owning a house slave, but she dreamed of hiring a cook some day when she married. *If there is anyone left to marry after this war is finally over,* she thought gloomily, letting out a sigh.

Glancing through the doorway at the table settings, Amara felt that familiar ache in her heart as she saw the empty spot where Michael normally sat. She hadn't seen him since he set off with his company after his last leave almost a year ago. They had received several brief missives from him since then, but the correspondence halted abruptly some three months ago. At first, Amara was confident he would resurface, but as time went on her optimism waned. She adored her oldest brother. He was talented and smart and witty. His friends from school were just like him and Amara secretly admired several of them. It hurt to think she would never see them all together again, at least not on this plane. *Now that's another dismal thought.* A shiver ran down her spine as she went back into the dining room and took her place at the table.

The rustling of skirts alerted the occupants of the room to Theresa's arrival. Amara could feel the headache she was nursing earlier start to pound its way back into her skull. *Wonderful, we get to hear another report of a carefree day spent perfecting the womanly skills acquired at the magnificent Lucy Cobb Institute*. It was aggravating enough that Theresa took her spot at the establishment when their families were united in marriage, but it was maddening listening to her constant prattling about it. With the war intensifying and business decreasing, Amara doubted her father could come up with the money to pay for her stepsister's autumn term, though. Theresa seemed oblivious to that possibility. The sense of satisfaction thinking the chit may get her comeuppance was temporary as the thought of living in close quarters with her year-round doused her spirits like icy water.

"*Bonjour, Maman*," exclaimed Theresa as she breezed through the doorway, planting a kiss on each side of her mother's face. "*Comment t'allez vous?*" she inquired, enunciating each syllable.

"I am doing wonderfully, *merci*. Seeing *ma belle fille* always brightens my day," said the proud mother, a smile lighting her face. "I see you're working on your French lessons. Anything else today?"

"*Oui, Maman*, you will never believe the marvelous stitch we learned at the institute last semester. I've been practicing it the entire day. It will be the finishing touch for the pillowcases I'm embroidering for my hope chest."

*Goodness gracious*, thought Amara, willing herself not to roll her eyes. *If filling up that bottomless trunk means Theresa will soon be making her own home, I am going to pick up my embroidery lessons where I left off three years ago and help her along in the process.* Now *that* is a marvelous idea, noted Amara thoughtfully as she got up from the table at her stepmother's bidding to fetch the sweet potatoes from the kitchen.

Theresa chattered on, recounting every minute detail of her day while the family took their seats and dishes were passed around the table. Amara was on the verge of spouting, "*Fermez la bouche*," when her father picked the opportune time to step in from his office. Neither McKirnan parent was fluent in French, but Theresa no doubt would have been more than willing to translate and inform them that Amara had told her in no uncertain terms to shut her mouth.

"Sorry te keep everyone waiting but I wanted te pencil the day's entries in the ledger prior te dinner," said Joseph McKirnan, his Irish brogue as thick as it was the day he set foot on American soil. He pulled out the chair at the head of the table and continued. "Quite the busy day. The house servants must have caught wind we received a shipment of muslin and linen. There was a line outside before I even opened up the doors. I could have used yer help, Amara."

A wave of guilt washed over Amara. "Father, if I would have known, I could have waited a day to start assisting Uncle William," she said earnestly.

"I have no doubt yer Uncle William needed ye much more than I did. I know there was a battle a few hours north of here the day before yesterday. I would imagine all the hospitals in town are filled te the brim." He was met with silence around the table. Seeing the need to change the subject, he turned towards his wife, "Shall we say grace, my dear?"

Amara dutifully bowed her head along with the others as her father paused before beginning the prayer. "In the name of the Father and of the Son and of the Holy Ghost...." She stole a sidelong glance at James sitting next to her. It hadn't taken long for the remedy to take effect. His head was bowed so low she could swear he was asleep. A sharp tap of her boot heel against his shin immediately brought him to attention.

"Amen," said James, snapping his head up.

With eyes narrowed, Amara's father momentarily scrutinized his youngest son. He picked up the meal prayer where he left off and when he finished he turned his attention to James. "Stocking up on the remedy again, are we?"

"No, sir," said James, his face reddening. "The walk home from Uncle William's depleted my energy, that's all, sir."

"Is that so?" He didn't sound convinced but continued. "I'll take yer word for that, James, I'm sure ye wouldn't be dishonest with yer own father, now would ye." James' face darkened to a shade nearly matching the beets steaming on the plate set before him.

Turning away from his son, he patted his wife's hand which was resting on the table. The ruby nestled in the wedding band she had inherited, or confiscated, as James was known to say, from the late Mrs. McKirnan gleamed in the early evening sunlight. "Let us eat this wonderful dinner me lovely wife has so graciously prepared. And Amara, when ye've finished cleaning up the kitchen, would ye be kind enough te check over the sales fer the day? If anything is amiss, ye'll be sure te catch it."

"Yes, Father. I would be happy to."

\*\*\*

After dinner, the family members went their separate ways, leaving the dining area in Amara's hands to straighten and prepare for the next day's meals. She really didn't mind cleaning, just about anything was preferable to cooking. In addition, it gave her a chance to sort through her thoughts. The silence was heavenly after the chaos of the hospital and Theresa's never-ending chit chat. They may be close in age, but that was all the two had in common. Theresa was the spitting image of her mother—a petite blonde with china blue eyes who was always the center of attention when young men were in the vicinity. It never ceased to amaze Amara that boys continued to flock around the girl once she actually opened her pouty little mouth to speak. After two sentences, Amara inevitably felt like running in the opposite direction. *Maybe those practiced puppy dog eyes and fluttering lashes actually did attract men?* Amara wrinkled her nose in disgust. She wouldn't give the time of day to any man who would be gullible enough to get caught in Theresa's spell.

But w*hat type of man would suit me,* wondered Amara as she worked on her chores. In her fantasies, she always dreamed of marrying one of Michael's classmates, even though she hadn't seen most of them since their graduation ceremony three years ago. The class of '62 was graduated with the class of '61 under orders issued by the War Department as so many students were leaving West Point when their home states withdrew from the Union. Michael's friends looked so handsome in their cadet gray uniforms and, as grown up as she tried to act, they still treated her like his kid sister. But they were so full of life and laughter she couldn't be angry with them if she tried.

As of this moment, Amara had no idea of any of their whereabouts or how they fared. The young men were scattered throughout the war-torn region. Talk circulated around town that several of them had taken up with the Union Army. That thought was too upsetting for Amara to even ponder. Her knowledge of political affairs was sparse, as men generally talked about such things behind closed doors, but she knew she could never associate with someone who fought on the side of the devil Ulysses S. Grant. According to her father, that man was hell-bent on destroying the South and taking away the rights of states to determine their own destiny. Having escaped from that sort of tyranny when he left Ireland, he wasn't keen to be saddled with that again in his adopted country.

She let out a sigh and, dismissing those thoughts, Amara finished tidying up and set to work checking over the sums for the day's sales. As her father mentioned, purchases of muslin and linen accounted for most of the take. Sales of whale bones, corsets and steel for hoop skirts were lagging, which reflected the uncertainty of the times. Citizens were on edge with talk of advancing Union forces having an eye on taking over Atlanta. The days of balls and dances were over until this act of aggression towards the South was squelched once and for all.

Amara could hear her father and stepmother in the parlor having their nightcap, her father no doubt enjoying his beloved Irish whiskey and Mrs. McKirnan a glass or two of sherry. Not once could Amara recall spirits passing her own mother's lips. Yet one more reason to question her father's thinking in choosing Mrs. McKirnan to be his new wife.

A thud from the sleeping quarters Amara shared with Theresa was a sure sign that her stepsister was working on her posture, albeit without much success. *That's a waste of a good book if I ever heard of one,* she thought wryly.

James was off doing Lord knew what. He reminded Amara of a tomcat, prowling about at night, always in search of something.

*Perhaps we're all in search of something,* considered Amara. Her thoughts meandered unbidden back to the hospital. The soldier with the grape shot wound was the finest-looking man Amara had ever laid eyes on. But good looks would only get a person so far. If his puzzling behavior wasn't due to a head injury, what would cause him to display such a sour disposition?

With a firm resolve to observe that particular gentleman more closely on the morrow, Amara turned her mind back to her father's books. A half-hour later, she finished up and started blowing out the candles on the first floor. Hearing a voice coming from the back room, she figured Theresa was either conversing with her reflection in the mirror or talking in her sleep, both common occurrences.

Amara stepped into the bedroom, where indeed her step-sister was asleep, and then started getting ready for bed herself. She stripped down to her shift and then pulled the pins out of her hair. Grabbing the brush off of her dresser, she tugged it through her hair, counting to one hundred by fives to shorten the process. *Good enough*, she thought before setting the brush down and twisting the hair into a figure eight so she could work the nightcap around the locks and pull the ties tight. She then settled into her side of the bed and paused to listen for a moment before pulling the ends of the pillow over her ears to drown out Theresa's voice.

As exhausted as she was, she slept fitfully, visions of a mysterious man haunting her dreams.

# Chapter III

The next day dawned bright and sunny. While it was invigorating for Amara, it didn't appear to have the same effect on James. He rolled away as Amara attempted to get him out of bed.

"Wake up, sleepyhead. Remember your promise to walk me to Uncle William's," prodded Amara as she tugged on his arm to roll him back. James squinted as he looked at her, apparently not comprehending why his slumber was being disrupted after so few hours of sleep.

Surveying her brother's dilated pupils and pale features, Amara couldn't refrain from admonishing him. "You're not looking good at all this morning."

"If I look anything like I feel, that would be an understatement, to be certain," said James in a raspy voice as he stretched his arms overhead and then slowly brought himself up to a sitting position. "I had a rather rough night of it." He tilted his head to each side to crack his neck. "I hate to say this, Sis, but I don't believe I am up to escorting you to the hospital this morning. Will Uncle William be in need of your services today?"

"As long as men are quartered in his house, I would say he will. But I am quite capable of making my way there on my own. Get some more sleep. You'll be back to your old self in no time."

"As appealing as that sounds, I will never be back to my *old* self," said James regretfully. "But I thank you for the reprieve. Walk straight to Uncle William's and keep your wits about you. I don't want you to be accosted by any thugs lurking the streets."

"No need to worry, James. All the hooligans will be holed up in the alleyways sleeping off their excesses. I will see you at the end of the day then?"

"I shall be there waiting to do your bidding, m'lady."

"Then I'm off. Take care of yourself while I'm gone and try to stay out of Mrs. McKirnan's way."

Amara departed from his bedroom and on her way through the kitchen grabbed the handkerchief holding biscuits for her noon meal. She had heard her father in the lower level of the house earlier but, since he had gone back upstairs, Amara decided to leave without making any more goodbyes.

Just as she was about to slip out the front door, she saw her father coming down the stairs. Amara took a glance past him to ensure her stepmother wasn't on his heels. Thankfully, Mrs. McKirnan was catching up on her beauty sleep, a never-ending quest. *She needs to keep her youthful appearance so she can get her claws into some other man if something were to happen to Father*, speculated Amara. The thought came to her mind before she could stop it. *God bless it! More fodder for confession this week.*

"Good mornin', Amara. Heading te the hospital so soon?"

"I am Father, and running a bit behind at that."

"I wanted te thank ye for yer work on the books last night. Everything seems te be in order and balanced te the penny, as per usual. Say hello te yer uncle for me when ye see him, will ye?"

"You are most welcome and I shall. I hope business goes smoothly for you today, Father."

With a wave, Amara headed out to the sidewalk and quickly started walking towards the hospital. It was a glorious morning, and the heady smell from the rhododendron bushes lining the path rejuvenated her.

Most of the neighborhood had yet to awaken. She picked up her cadence as she started to hum *I Wish I Was in Dixie Land*. On such a day as this, a person could forget there was a war being waged just beyond the boundaries of the city. Aside from the fact that most of the homes flew Rebel flags, the town looked much as it had four years earlier.

As she anticipated, Amara arrived at her destination without incident. Mentally bracing herself, she climbed the stairs to the front door and let herself in. As much as she wanted to hurry up the stairs to the ward, she couldn't help but pause to take a glance into the parlor. Poking her head around the doorframe, her nostrils were assaulted with a god-awful smell that made her eyes burn. An eerie calm engulfed the area. There were a good number of empty cots but her attention was riveted to the ones that were occupied. Amara's heart leapt to her throat when she saw bodies draped head to toe with sheets. The memory of her mother's corpse covered in a similar fashion immediately sprang to mind. Try as she might, Amara could not move. She was rooted to the floor.

"We did everything we could for them," said Doc, gently placing his hand on Amara's shoulder. "Their suffering has ended."

Speaking was difficult with the lump lodged in her throat. "I will say a prayer for the repose of their souls," Amara managed to stammer.

"That's all anyone can do at this point. The good news is, a number of men have been moved to the ballroom. Their prognosis is much brighter. I am sure meeting you will improve their spirits as well."

"Then I shall attend to them immediately, Uncle," said Amara, averting her eyes from the cots and their lifeless occupants as she turned from the doorway.

"Amara, the young man you inquired about, his noggin is perfectly intact, just as I suspected it would be."

"Really?

Her uncle looked at her quizzically, one eyebrow raised.

"I mean, that certainly is good to hear," said Amara in a rush.

She turned away and quickly began to ascend the stairs. *Intact for now, but it will be an entirely different matter if he doesn't mind his behavior around me in the future,* she thought, vividly recalling his rudeness the day before.

Entering the ballroom, Amara saw that there were indeed new patients, but was disturbed to notice that some of the men she met yesterday were missing. Considering the severity of their injuries, that realization did not bode well. She scanned the room and saw the Texan in the back corner fast asleep, his bandaged chest rising and falling in a steady rhythm. A sense of relief flooded over her. *Praise God!* As ill-mannered as he may have been, she wanted nothing more for him than she wanted for all the soldiers in their care: a full recovery. He was a Confederate soldier and his services, like those of most every able-bodied man, were sorely needed on the battlefield to secure victory for the Confederacy.

Amara started her rounds by greeting the new arrivals. She was determined to make their stay in the hospital as pleasant as possible, considering this could be the last stop on their earthly journey.

The hours passed quickly as Amara devoted as much time as she felt she could to each man. The newcomers' requests were similar to the ones she had honored the day before—a bit of conversation, letters home or a hand to hold. Prayers were offered for the men, their departed brothers in arms and their loved ones.

Having been raised in a devout Catholic home, Amara was adept at rattling off prayers in Latin she had been reciting her entire life. Those weren't necessarily the words the men were looking to hear. They all professed to be

Christian—war has a tendency to bring piety out in folks, Amara noticed—but they walked different paths. Conversing in a casual style was the way most of the soldiers communicated with the Lord. At first, praying in that fashion was a bit awkward for Amara, but she felt more at ease as she went along. She was glad to be able to bring the men a sense of peace.

Amara stopped to visit with several of the men she met previously. Thankfully, most of them seemed to be healing properly. She couldn't help but look towards the Texan when she was on his end of the room, but he was oblivious to her as he was lost in slumber. Or so she thought.

\*\*\*

Nathan sensed her presence almost as soon as she walked into the room. Unlike several of the other soldiers he noticed who were overtly surveying her every move, he watched her through veiled lashes, feigning sleep as she made her rounds. It had been a few months since he laid eyes on a respectable female—and a fetching one at that, but he was perplexed as to why she was helping out at the hospital.

He had categorized her as a typical Southern miss when he first saw her the day before, either making a benevolent show of visiting a few wounded soldiers so she could boast to her friends that she had been inside an actual hospital or perhaps embarking on a mission to save souls from eternal damnation. But the fact that she came back for a second day said something about her character. The more Nathan observed Amara, the more he realized he may have been hasty in his judgment.

As far as he could determine, she wasn't hell bent on evangelizing the flock before her. There was no wedding ring on her left hand, yet she showed no interest in trolling for a husband from the rapidly diminishing pool the war had left behind. She genuinely seemed to care about the men she met. *Could any female really be that altruistic,* he wondered. From his experience, Southern women were masters at manipulation. Their dealings with men, particularly eligible ones, were calculated to obtain their desires, which in most cases was a golden noose to put around an unsuspecting chap's neck. He wanted nothing to do with any of them.

Trying to shake the chit from his thoughts, he turned his head back and willed himself to get more rest. Mistress Amara may not be on a mission but he certainly was, and it was going to take every ounce of energy and ingenuity he had to complete it.

Within a few minutes, he fell asleep and loosened his grip on present time. He went back to a day some nine years earlier.

*February 26, 1855*

*His mother had given birth to another baby girl. Her previous deliveries had been difficult because of her slight build and fragile health but, with her indomitable spirit, she had always recovered in due time. Through the years one babe was lost, but eight pregnancies ended successfully.*

*With his older sister married and living away from home, Nathan was in charge of running the house and watching over his two younger brothers and four sisters when his mother had come to term. While she labored, he occupied the youngsters to keep them away from her sleeping quarters. God forbid they disturb her and raise their father's ire.*

*His father, Edward Robert Simmons, was a God-fearing man and a pillar in their community. He was known throughout Massachusetts for his prowess in* business—having systematically built a thriving corporation in Lowell over a twenty-year time span. Everything in his life was structured—from his weapons manufacturing facility to his household.

He expected his wife to bear their newest offspring, recuperate accordingly, and be back on her feet within seven days to resume her tasks of raising the children and running the household.

However, things didn't appear to be going as planned.

Nathan sensed something was wrong with this delivery. The physician stayed in his parents' room for nearly two hours after the birth, leading him to believe the newborn was having difficulties. The arrival of the priest confirmed his suspicions. His siblings knew something was amiss, but didn't comprehend the gravity of the situation. At Nathan's urging, the older children prayed the rosary in unison for their baby sister, offering a lifetime of exemplary behavior in exchange for her survival.

No one was allowed in the master bedroom, save their father, the reverend and the attending physician. When the doctor finally walked out of the room, snapping his satchel closed, Nathan felt a sense of trepidation. His fears were well-grounded as his father followed shortly afterwards, a grim look on his face.

"We've lost her," said his father.

Nathan nodded and said with empathy, "We'll pray for her little soul."

"I'm referring to your mother, boy."

Nathan's eyes widened in disbelief. The droning sound of a swarm of angry bees began to build in his head and the room splintered into bright bits of light before his eyes.

"You may go in and say your farewells if you like," said his father gruffly. "The babe is gone as well."

*Noticing Nathan's stricken look, he added, "I don't want to see any tears from you. You're fifteen years old and nearly a grown man. You need to set an example for your younger brothers."*

*Nodding mechanically, Nathan turned away and walked into the darkened room, the youngsters crowding behind him. The priest stepped aside and the children surrounded the bed where their mother laid, her arms tightly wrapped around an angelic infant. The pair looked as though they were peacefully slumbering. The little ones clamored to get near their beloved mother. Tears stung his eyes but Nathan stoically held them back as sobbing began to build in earnest around him.*

*He started to keel back and forth and then dropped to the floor.*

That sensation jerked Nathan wide awake. To his surprise he wasn't lying on the ground but rather on a bed of some sort. As his eyes darted around the room, he knew he was in a familiar setting and realized he had been dreaming again. His heart raced and his skin was damp from perspiration.

Noticing a young lady bent over a cot not four rows from his own, he let out a shaky sigh and closed his eyes again until he could quiet his breathing.

\*\*\*

Amara approached the last man on her agenda for the morning. *Good Lord,* thought Amara. *How old could this boy be?* While most of the soldiers were in need of a good shave, this one barely had peach fuzz covering his chin.

"Hello," said Amara, settling herself on the edge of his cot. "This might sound a bit forward, but may I ask how old you are?"

"Ma'am, I ain't so sure of the day, but come September I'm gonna be fourteen."

A look of astonishment flashed across Amara's face. *Thirteen years old?* She quickly composed herself. "Well, what do you know? September is my birth month as well, though I'm fairly certain I was born on the second day of the month because I saw the inscription in our family Bible. So you are thirteen," stated Amara. "How in the name of heaven did you end up in the middle of a battle? You should be back home working on your studies, not fighting a war."

"Ma'am, I weren't lookin' to get myself shot. When my brother joined up, I snuck out after him with my Pa's bugle. Figured I knew enough notes to make a bugler for my brother's company. By the time Paulie found out I had followed him, it was too late to send me back."

"Your mother must be worried sick about you."

"Don't rightly know she's figured out I'm missin' yet. She's got a passel of young'uns to look after. 'Course Paulie says they're sending me back home soon's I mend up. I ain't too sure who I'm more afeared of—the Yanks or my ma. She's gonna smack me upside the head when I git there."

"I am sure she'll be grateful to see you again." Amara smiled at the thought. "Is there something I can do for you while I'm here?"

"Been thinkin' a bit 'bout my ma since I been layin' here. She don't take no guff from us kids but she got herself a soft side too. She'd tuck the babies in at night and sing 'til they's asleep. Kinda miss hearin' her warblin'." Casting his eyes downward, he continued. "Don't want to sound like no sissy but, if you could do a note or two, I'd be mighty grateful."

"You want me to sing?"

"Yes, Ma'am. If that ain't askin' too much."

"No, not at all," said Amara as she surreptitiously

glanced over to the cot holding the Texan. *Lost to the world. Let's hope he's a sound sleeper.*

A song came to Amara's head. Her father couldn't carry a tune in a basket, but he would sing this song with gusto when he was in his cups, thinking back to the days of his youth on the Emerald Isle.

Amara cleared her throat and softly began to sing.

> The Minstrel Boy to the war is gone
> In the ranks of death you will find him;
> His father's sword he hath girded on,
> And his wild harp slung behind him;
> "Land of Song!" said the warrior bard,
> "Tho' all the world betrays thee,
> One sword, at least, thy rights shall guard,
> One faithful harp shall praise thee!"
>
> The Minstrel fell! But the foeman's chain
> Could not bring that proud soul under;
> The harp he lov'd ne'er spoke again,
> For he tore its chords asunder;
> And said "No chains shall sully thee,
> Thou soul of love and brav'ry!
> Thy songs were made for the pure and free,
> They shall never sound in slavery!"

Encouraged by the adoring look the young boy cast upon her, Amara continued, her pure tone and heartfelt rendering of the song drawing the attention of most of the occupants of the room.

> The Minstrel Boy will return we pray
> When we hear the news we all will cheer it,
> The minstrel boy will return one day,
> Torn perhaps in body, not in spirit.
> Then may he play on his harp in peace,
> In a world such as Heaven intended,

> For all the bitterness of man must cease,
> And ev'ry battle must be ended.

As the last note echoed away, a smattering of applause sounded in the room. Breaking from her reverie, Amara felt the color rising in her cheeks. She acknowledged her admirers with a nod and a thank you.

Glancing down at the boy, she saw him struggling to keep his eyes open. Within a few seconds, he drifted off to sleep and she slipped away from his side. Amara had the sensation that someone was staring right through her. She turned to see the Texan assessing her, his steel gray eyes hooded by long, dark lashes. He was flushed with fever but his voice was unwavering as he addressed her.

"The Minstrel Boy? Were you meaning to cheer him up or lead him to believe his days were numbered?" queried the man with a hint of amusement in his voice.

"It was the first song that came to my head," stammered Amara. "It's a fine Irish song, I'll have you know," she said, tilting her chin up.

"It seems an odd song for a Southern miss to be singing, seeing that Meagher's Irish Brigade has adopted it for their own. 'Meagher be wearing the blue, don't ye know,'" added the Texan in a feigned Irish accent.

"For your information, I learned that song at my father's knee. 'There be Irish in Georgia, don't ye know,'" shot back Amara, her ire beginning to show. "And they not be kissin' Grant's hairy arse for that matter, either," she hissed. With that, Amara swept from the room, the sounds of the corporal's laughter ringing in her ears.

# Chapter IV

As the week wore on, men were shipped back to their units or, for those no longer fit for service, off to the train station to make their way back home. Amara avoided talking to Corporal Simmons, ashamed of herself for letting him get the best of her and making her lose her temper—a venial sin, but a sin nonetheless. The thought of confessing what she had said to the priest humiliated her to the very marrow of her bones.

Although she tried to keep her distance from him, she was constantly aware of the man's presence. As bothersome as it was, for some reason she was drawn to him. His handsome features could take any girl's breath away, but Amara knew she wasn't like other girls. Her father always said she had a good head on her shoulders— she would have made a fine business owner had she been born a male. She was adept at maintaining focus on the important things at hand and, at this moment, that meant helping mend the spirits of the broken soldiers at the hospital—not mooning over some corporal who didn't give a hoot about her.

Not that the man would notice in the state he was in. The fever that had come upon the corporal raged on, and he fell in and out of consciousness. Amara was concerned for him, but her uncle assured her that a fever was actually a good sign—it indicated his body was fighting off infection.

Several times in the last few days when she knew Corporal Simmons was lost in some distant world, Amara held cool compresses to his head, quietly speaking heartening words or singing softly to him—purposely omitting the ruinous minstrel boy song from her repertoire.

As she performed her ministrations, her guard slid down somewhat and she had more charitable feelings toward him. It started when she discovered the crucifix he had tried concealing from her the first time they met. The gold pendant shone brightly against the dingy sheet covering his chest. Picking it up and rubbing the textured gold piece between her fingers, Amara felt a kinship with him that she hadn't before.

Throughout the week, she created various scenarios in her mind that could explain his initial behavior. Maybe a comrade died in his arms or he lost a brother on the battlefield. Maybe he's just as worn out and scared as anyone else in his situation would be. *Who am I to judge him?* Drawing the washcloth over his forehead to smooth out the furrows in his brow, her thoughts meandered on. *War has a way of hardening men's hearts.*

\*\*\*

Feeling a gentle hand upon his face, Nathan thought his mama was at his bedside. *Can it be?* He attempted to open his eyes but they would not budge no matter how hard he tried. Bits and pieces from the past swirled through his mind. To his sorrow, he remembered attending his mother's wake and funeral service.

*March 1, 1855*
*He had gone through the motions of greeting their neighbors and friends, accepting their condolences stone-faced. When the day finally ended, his father pulled him aside.*

*"As you know, son, I have my hands full running the factory. I have neither the time nor the patience to properly look after seven children," said the man in a matter-of-fact tone. "I've summoned your older sister and*

*she is on her way here as we speak. Mary Louise and her husband have agreed to take over responsibility for the lot of you."*

*"Are you saying we are to live with her and Jacob? Are they moving back here?"*

*His father shook his head in exasperation. "You will be residing with them on their land in Illinois," he responded. Looking at his son sternly, he finished his thought. "You've got more than nine years of schooling under your belt. It's time you start earning your keep. You will be working on the ranch with your brother-in-law."*

*Countless thoughts came to Nathan's mind. Dropping out of school would be no hardship for him. He had enough book learning for one lifetime—sitting in a classroom was tedious and he was forever getting in trouble out of sheer boredom. An avid reader, he was convinced he was better educated than most of his instructors anyway. But leaving behind the life he had always known, his friends, the house filled with memories of his mother—it was more than he could face.*

*"Father, can't I stay here with you and work in the factory? I'm a quick learner and I will labor as hard, if not harder, than any of the men you have under your employ."*

*"That is absolutely out of the question," said his father with no hesitation. "I will not put your life at risk toiling in that environment. When you have the maturity and ability to manage other men, you will be trained for my position. Until that time, you will assist your sister and Jacob. Do I make myself clear?"*

*"Yes, sir," replied Nathan dejectedly.*

*Silence hung between them for several moments as his father shifted his weight from toe to heel several times before digging his right hand into his overcoat pocket.*

"Son?"

"Yes, sir," *Nathan replied, eyes downcast.*

*His father was uncharacteristically hesitant. "As you are my oldest male child, I have something I want to give you," he said, pulling his hand out of his pocket.*

*Uncurling his fingers, a gold ring was revealed. Nathan instantly recognized the piece. "Your mother wanted you to have this."*

*Nathan gently took hold of the band, realizing it was the first time he had seen it anywhere other than on his mother's left hand. He couldn't stem the flow of tears as he felt the smooth surface. Memories of her rushed through his mind.*

*"Thank you, sir," was all he could manage to choke out.*

\*\*\*

The sound of a bucket hitting the floor jolted Nathan awake the next morning. He turned his head to the right and saw Amara across the room, her hair held back with a scarf, bending down to dip a horsehair brush in the water. She began to methodically scrub the wooden planks for all she was worth.

Nathan had to smile seeing how absorbed she was in her work. She certainly put her heart and soul into everything she did. What little time he had been awake the last few days, he had been studying her—both attending her duties and interacting with the other soldiers. She made it a point to thank each man for his service to the Confederacy. When she sat by a bedside, her entire attention was focused on the man in front of her. She genuinely did seem to care about the patients. He could honestly say he had never met a young lady like her before—one just as lovely on the inside as the outside. *She's a gem all right.*

In a different place and a different time, he'd do whatever he could to convince her to be his girl. But try as he might, he couldn't imagine even one scenario where that would be possible under the present circumstances. He'd have to content himself with all the memories of her he could etch into his brain before their paths diverged.

\*\*\*

Being that it was the last day of the work week and there were fewer men to attend to, Amara focused on scrubbing the ballroom floor in its entirety before day's end. She ascribed to her mother's dictum that cleanliness was next to godliness, and was going about her heavenly duties with vigor.

She was working her way from the doorway to the far end of the room. Amara was grateful she wore her simple gray gown rather than the burdensome hoops the fashionable ladies in town were sporting. *Why anyone would aspire to look like a Paris socialite in the middle of a war zone is beyond me,* thought Amara as she attacked the stained floor, slopping dirty water along the hem of her dress as she went.

As she scrubbed, Amara's mind wandered back through the week, recalling some of the men they had lost—the young man with a newborn son he yearned to meet for the first time, the older gentleman anxious to hear news of his boys who had been caught in a crossfire, the newlywed looking forward to returning to his wife—"the purdiest gal this side o' the Mississippi," the preacher preparing to lead his flock again. It was heartbreaking to think of them, knowing that their dreams would never be fulfilled. Amara grieved as each man slipped away. She held the father's hand as he struggled for his last breath, assuring him she would do whatever it took to locate his sons and tell them that their pa was proud of them and his last wish was for their health and safety.

As Amara neared the end of the room, a trail of gleaming wood in her wake, a movement from under one of the cots caught her eye. In a flash the scrub brush went flying, Amara was off the floor and huddled on the nearest cot.

"Jesus, Mary, Joseph," exclaimed Amara, crossing herself with a shaking hand.

A snake slithered past the bed, taking a leisurely path to the open veranda doors. Amara let out a sigh of relief that was cut short when she realized upon whose cot she knelt. She began inching her way towards the foot of the bed in as nonchalant a manner as she could muster.

"Do you often join men in their beds, Miss McKirnan?" asked the Texan solicitously.

Amara's cheeks burned. "I do not make a habit of it, trust me. Can't you see that snake over there?"

"It looks harmless to me," said Nathan as he watched the creature make its getaway.

"Harmless? Don't you know a copperhead when you see one?" asked Amara incredulously.

"Well... if it's like any other snake, I'm sure he was just as afraid of you as you were of him," said Nathan with an air of authority.

Amara shook her head in disbelief. *That reptile may not have been full grown, but how could he not recognize the distinctive pattern on its skin?* She leaned forward and put the back of her hand to Nathan's forehead. He looked at her expectantly. "Well, the fever has broken, but you may still be a bit addled."

Reluctant to leave her safe perch, Amara had an idea. "Seeing that you're awake now, why don't you get up and take a peek under the other cots to be sure your friend hasn't left any relatives behind. Then I can be on my way."

"You would ask a grievously wounded soldier to do such a laborious task?" inquired the corporal with mock surprise.

"Grievously wounded, my foot. I know every man left in this ward is being shipped back to their units this afternoon and, now that your fever is gone, you'll be leaving with the rest of the lot. A little walking and bending would be good for you. And while you're at it, you may want to borrow my scrub brush and work on the spots I missed."

Rolling to his side, Nathan gingerly pushed himself up to a sitting position. He paused for a bit, then leaned forward and slowly rose to a standing position. Once on his feet, he cautiously took one step, then another. With a stiff gait, he slowly walked around the cots encircling his own, giving a cursory glance under each one.

"I would say the area is secured, Ma'am."

"Thank you, sir."

"I should be the one thanking you," said Nathan, growing serious. "You've been a godsend to these soldiers this week. I am sure they will always remember you with fondness."

Amara gave him a guarded look as he continued. "Thank you as well for sharing your singing talents. I could almost hear the bagpipes in the background as you went along."

*What is it about me that men have such a penchant for teasing me,* fumed Amara, as she saw the smile threatening the corner of his lips. *He's just like Michael's friends.* She countered his remark. "Am I to understand you're a bagpipe enthusiast? Do they even have such a thing in Texas, sir?"

"I've yet to see one. Let it suffice to say they are a childhood memory for me," said Nathan, lowering himself onto his cot. Amara cocked her head and looked at him, waiting for further explanation.

None was forthcoming. "I should let you get back to your duties and I'll attend to mine as well," said Nathan matter-of-factly. "If we're being shipped out this afternoon,

I'll need to gather my belongings. Take care of yourself."

"And you as well. You will be in my prayers to Saint Adrian," said Amara earnestly.

"Ah, the patron saint of soldiers. I shall be in good form with him watching my head," quipped Nathan.

"The good saint may be watching your head, sir, but you need to keep it low if you want it to remain attached to your shoulders. If ever I were to meet you again, I would prefer it be outside these hospital walls."

A look briefly crossed Nathan's face that Amara was unable to decipher. "I shall do my best to make it through the rest of this conflict unscathed," said Nathan, his gray eyes looking directly into her deep blue ones.

Amara got off the cot and started inching away, unable to break his gaze. When she stumbled into the bucket the trance finally broke.

"Fair enough," she stammered, bending down to pick up the container. She straightened up as regally as she could and gave the Texan one last brief look.

"Good bye, Corporal Simmons."

"Farewell, Miss McKirnan."

Amara turned away so he wouldn't see her chin quivering and beat a rapid retreat from the room. *Will I ever see him again? Will I ever see any of these men again?* Unshed tears burned the back of her throat. *What fate awaits them? What fate awaits all of us?* With a heavy heart, Amara hurried down the stairs. She wanted to be tucked into the farthest corner of the hospital when the men left. She wasn't one for goodbyes, especially when, as of late, too many of them were forever.

# Chapter V

Nathan joined the throng of fellow soldiers milling around the train station. Schedules were sporadic at best these days so the time the next train would pull in was anyone's guess. He was not looking forward to rejoining his brigade, but at least by boarding the train he would be moving somewhere. The heat was stifling and bodies filled every square inch of the enclosure. Like himself, most of the men were heading back to rejoin their units which, from what he gleaned from their conversations, were scattered throughout the northern part of the state.

Several hours passed before a train finally chugged into the station. A few civilians disembarked, but the majority of the passengers were military personnel. Anxious wives and family members scanned the travelers, searching for familiar faces. Some of the soldiers looked to be in fairly good shape so they could be on leave, assuming leaves were still being granted. But most of them were sporting injuries. Whether they were being discharged from active military service and heading back to their hometowns or getting admitted to the local infirmaries, it was hard to say. Men hobbled off the train with crutches, some were carried off atop makeshift stretchers, and the rest were supported by fellow servicemen who looked to be in rather sorry states themselves.

*The hospitals in this city should never lack for customers,* mused Nathan as he observed the motley group filling the platform. His thoughts turned to Amara, as he considered what she may be doing at that very moment. He couldn't shake her from his mind. *Maybe I truly am addled.*

As Nathan inched up to the platform, he recalled the

other inhabitants of the hospital eyeing Amara up—from the seasoned soldiers with leering visages to the young pups with unchecked admiration. He felt protective of her. One may even say jealous, if that were an emotion to which he ascribed. Had he been up to it, he would have taught the lot of them a lesson on how to treat a lady properly. *As if I'm authority on that,* thought Nathan ruefully as he recalled their initial encounter.

But really, he couldn't blame the other soldiers. Who wouldn't want to gaze at that girl? Lord knows there was little else to keep the men occupied. Pictures flashed through his mind of the past week. He saw Amara compassionately tending to patients...working until she could hardly stand on her feet...sitting on a window seat clutching her rosary when she had a free moment...biting her lip and tucking her hair behind her ears when she felt distraught. *Some fine Confederate soldier will have himself a catch when he puts a ring on that little lady's finger.*

Attempting to shake her from his mind, Nathan turned his attention to jostling his way through the crowd to board the train. He made his way to the back of the coach, dropped his haversack to the floor and settled into the seat adjacent to the window. He pulled his slouch hat low over his eyes.

Filled to overflowing, with stragglers packing the aisles, the train eventually jerked into motion. Pretending to be sleeping to avoid conversing with the soldier who had settled in next to him, Nathan let his thoughts drift as the locomotive gained speed.

*How did I ever get myself entangled in this mess in the first place,* Nathan asked himself as they moved away from the city. Glancing down at his gray uniform trousers, he shook his head in disgust. *What would Father think if he could see me now?*

At this point, who knew if his father was dead or alive. Running a munitions factory during peacetime was stressful enough for a driven person like him. Keeping up with production for the war effort may have been enough to kill him.

As the train chugged northward, the mesmerizing rhythm of the vehicle set Nathan's mind to wandering once again.

*March 18, 1855*

*Nathan saw Mary Louise standing on the train platform ready to shepherd him and their younger siblings halfway across the country to her and Jacob's ranch. She was only 17 years old herself and was not much bigger than their mother. Nathan imagined this would be a large burden for her to take on. Not that she had any choice in the matter. When their father issued a command, everyone obeyed—resistance was a futile exercise as Nathan had learned the hard way as a youngster. His backside still hurt just thinking about it.*

*The train they all boarded meandered its way from Massachusetts to Connecticut, New York, Pennsylvania, Ohio, Indiana and finally Illinois. Nathan felt the life he once knew slipping further away with each mile. After three days, the train reached Chicago where the entourage was greeted by their brother-in-law. Everyone piled onto the buckboard to ride the forty miles southwest to the homestead in Tonica.*

*Thus a new chapter had begun for Nathan. Aspiring to make his father proud, he threw himself into work on the ranch, learning everything he could about raising cattle, growing and rotating crops, maintaining buildings, and negotiating prices. Mary Louise took care of Adele and Frances while David, Anne, Stephen and Ruth attended school.*

*The hard work and time outdoors did wonders for Nathan. Not only did the pain of losing his mother gradually fade, but he grew overnight from a scrawny youth to a tall and muscular young man with a love for wide open spaces. When school was out for summer, David and Stephen helped on the ranch while Ruth and Anne took care of the house and their younger sisters, giving some much-needed relief to Mary Louise who was carrying her first child.*

*By the end of June the decision was made to expand the operation of the ranch, so Jacob set about finding more help. Providence landed a fellow by the name of Dominic Warner on their doorstep one late summer day. The young man, only a few months older than Nathan, had recently lost both of his parents in a house fire. Dominic offered his brawn to farmers and ranchers for days or weeks at a time and when he no longer was needed, moved on. Thus he arrived at the Green homestead, all of his worldly possessions tied up in a handkerchief hanging from the pole he carried over his shoulder.*

*Nathan respected Dominic. While he didn't have much schooling, this sharecropper's son was intelligent and had a way with words. Being of German descent, he was short and stocky and as strong as an ox. He quickly proved to be an asset to his employer both in the field and at the open market.*

*As the two young men worked side-by-side, they hatched a plan to buy their own ranch. By the time Nathan reached the age of majority in July of 1858, the pair had a solid course of action laid out. From what Nathan could determine, the days of ranching in Illinois were numbered. More families were flooding in from the East and land was getting harder to come by. His brothers and sisters were settled in their lives with Mary*

*Louise and Jacob and so Nathan felt it was time to pursue his own dreams.*

*Nathan and Dominic set their sights on Texas, a land so vast they believed it would forever be uncluttered by civilization.*

# Chapter VI

Amara spent the rest of the day up in the ballroom giving the place a good airing out. She collected soiled bandages to be washed and stripped sheets from beds. When she went to gather the bedding from Nathan's cot, she couldn't help but bunch it up by her face to take in his scent. A feeling of downheartedness washed over her.

Such a fine looking man, the thought of him being marred at the hands of the enemy was dismaying. *Wasn't there a better way for two sides to settle their differences than by pitting their young men against each other to the death?* It all seemed so noble and glamorous before Amara had started helping at the hospital. Now it was beginning to seem pointless.

A drawn out sigh escaped from her lips. It was understandable that she was dispirited after spending a week surrounded by the dead and dying. Yet, even engulfed in that misery she had tried to maintain a sense of hope. These soldiers were fighting to save the rights of the Southern people. They had just cause, did they not? For those whose lives slipped away at the hospital, Father O'Reilly was there to hear their confessions and administer the sacrament of Extreme Unction, so she knew they were bound for heaven.

A fair number of the patients would make full recoveries, Amara was certain of that. When this unpleasantness was behind them, they would return home and resume their lives once again. Several of the men she had met were as charming as they were good looking, and two or three vowed they would come back to the hospital someday to make her acquaintance in a more formal manner.

While she was flattered by the attention, it was inconsequential to her. She couldn't shake the Texan's visage from her memory. Thoughts of him intensified the hurt that permeated her very soul.

Amara knew her mother was looking down at her from heaven, but she wished she was standing before her this very moment. *What is wrong with me? Why do I care anything for a man whom I know so little about and in all likelihood will never see again?* She listened for a response, but all she heard was the buzzing of the tree frogs outside the open doors as they warmed up for their nightly chorus.

\*\*\*

From his window seat, Nathan was being serenaded as well. Dusk was settling over the land as the conductor announced their final destination. The trip north from Atlanta had been a tedious one. The jerking of the train aggravated his wounds, despite the linen tightly wrapped around his midsection. The vehicle stopped every hour to take on more passengers or undergo inspection by Rebel troops. Nathan surmised they were searching for deserters. He hunched down lower in his seat. *No use letting them get a good look at my face. Someday I may be one of the men for whom they're searching.*

It was somewhat ironic for Nathan that he could be ensconced in such intrigue—he was always the steadfast one, minding his own business, keeping his nose to the grindstone. He began sorting through the events that led him to the web in which he found himself entangled. It was actually quite the story when he thought about it.

*March 9, 1859*
*Nathan and Dominic had determined to start on their trek south when spring finally came to Illinois. There was*

*still a nip of winter in the air the day they saddled two of Jacob's palominos, but the sun shone brightly overhead. The saddlebags were bulging with food and gear for the trip.*

*Mary Louise, holding her squirming daughter on her hip, had tears in her eyes as she watched their final preparations.*

*"Nathan, for some reason, if things don't work out, you will always be welcome here," she said with a catch in her voice.*

*"I appreciate that, Mary Louise," Nathan replied. "But there's no turning back for me now. It's time to create my own place in this world. I truly thank both you and Jacob for taking all of us in. You're doing a fine job raising the children."*

*Mary Louise blushed at the compliment.*

*"Jacob," he added, shaking his brother-in-law's hand, "You are the older brother I never had. I've learned everything I know about ranching from you. I can't thank you enough."*

*"You want to show your thanks, Nathan? Make that ranch a success," replied Jacob.*

*"I will do that, Jacob. Mark my words."*

*Nathan shook his brothers' hands, strapping young men themselves now, and challenged them to step up and take his place on the ranch. A hug and a kiss on the cheek were administered to each of his little sisters and his niece, who by this time had managed to wiggle out of her mother's arms.*

*After Dominic said his goodbyes and expressed his gratitude as well, the pair was off.*

*They had mapped out a route southwest through Illinois to Missouri. A pace of thirty miles per day should be bearable for the horses and bring them to the Gateway to the West on the banks of the Mississippi within a week's time.*

*St. Louis was a sight to behold. The streets teemed with horse-drawn vehicles and people from every walk of life. Soldiers, businessmen, sailors, the well-heeled folks, street urchins and women of questionable repute all made their way through Lafayette Square. Nathan and Dominic opted to spend two days there, exploring the city and resting up for the remaining leg of their trip.*

*Further south the terrain changed and the climate improved considerably.*

*"Weather this nice this early in the year makes a fellow a bit jittery," commented Dominic as their horses kept up the steady pace through the prairie lands of southern Missouri. "Seems like tornados can spring up without so much as a 'How do you do.'" His eyes scanned the horizon, looking for telltale signs of a storm.*

*Nathan could feel the tension in the horse beneath him as if she sensed a storm brewing as well. "There aren't too many places to hide on this land," he noted, looking around him.*

*"Maybe we'll come across more caves like we found before," offered Dominic. "We'd find safe haven in one of those."*

*"If a bear with the same idea isn't already residing in it," said Nathan with a laugh. "Seriously though, keep your eyes open, you never know when we'll have to run for cover."*

*"Jacob gave us some fine horses, but I don't think even these fillies can outrun a twister," noted Dominic.*

*"Let's hope we never have to test that theory."*

*While the pair did see their share of downpours, they managed to stay out of the path of tornados. Stretched out on their bedrolls under the starry skies, Nathan and Dominic spent their nights talking about the future. The first priority once they were on their own land was to break ground for a house. Living outdoors was acceptable when the weather was temperate, but would grow cold quickly when the winter winds swept across the plains of Texas.*

*Each night after Dominic drifted off to sleep, Nathan stayed awake clutching the crucifix around his neck. It was dear to him as his mother had given it to him the day he was confirmed. He lamented the fact that he hadn't been able to attend Mass since they left Illinois, so he conducted a service inside his head every evening. The entire Mass played out until the final benediction or as far as he could remember before he fell asleep, his fingers still intertwined around the cross.*

*By the time the men reached the capital of Arkansas, they were three weeks into their expedition with a third of the way still ahead of them. Little Rock offered rooming houses with soft beds and warm meals, just what a body needed after so many days on the road. Nathan purchased a current edition of the Arkansas Gazette and read it out loud from cover to cover, giving Dominic a chance to hear about the latest news across the world.*

*Supplies were purchased before they set out again. The two decided to skirt around Indian territory to avoid trouble in that disputed area. The second week of May they reached their destination.*

*Grayson County looked to be the most promising area to purchase land for ranching in Texas. There was plenty of open space and as the Red River formed the northern border, there was access to water for animals and crops. Several families had given ranching a try and found the work to be more than they anticipated. Their departure left a number of parcels for newcomers looking to make their fortune taming the land.*

*The courthouse in Sherman, the county seat, handled all land transactions. Anxious to see Texas settled, the United States government was practically giving the abandoned land away. For a thousand dollars, Nathan was able to purchase nearly two hundred and fifty acres of land in the northwest corner of the county.*

*Stocking the ranch was Nathan's and Dominic's first concern. They spent a week in Sherman purchasing supplies they would need over the next few months. Fifty head of cattle were acquired at the weekly auction. The Texas Longhorns seemed the most logical choice for their purposes since the beasts could withstand droughts, heat, cold and disease.*

*A cow, some chickens, a sow and boar were added to their fold to supply fresh milk, eggs and eventually meat. Kitchen goods and sacks of flour and salt were tossed into the wagon they acquired from a local merchant.*

*A white American Paint with dark markings caught Nathan's eye in the Sherman stable yard. It was the ideal horse for patrolling the property and running the cattle. Dominic decided on the same breed for himself.*

*The filly Nathan chose was a spirited one. She nipped at him when he attempted to inspect her teeth. Thinking back to his studies of Greek mythology, the name Isis sprang to mind. That particular goddess had the task of teaching women how to tame men enough to live with them. Either I'm going to tame her or she's going to tame me, Nathan thought with amusement.*

*A Border collie was given to them by the gentleman who had the horses. The pup was christened Checkers for the black and white pattern in his fur.*

*It took nearly two days to get the animals and supplies to their land. Rounding up young steer with an inexperienced dog and newly-broken horses was a learning experience for the humans as well as the animals.*

*After months of preparation and travel, it was a gratifying moment riding onto their property for the first* time. *A grove of trees ran along the eastern edge. Nathan recognized maples, box elders and some fruit and nut species. The bulk of their property was littered with Texas Bluebonnets, daisies and a host of other perennials.*

*The words to a long-forgotten childhood song came to Nathan as he surveyed the terrain. "This truly is a world such as heaven intended," he proclaimed as he took it all in.*

*"Heavenly Vista Ranch—how does that strike you Dominic?"*

*"If that names sits well with you, it works for me too."*

*"Then that it is," proclaimed Nathan firmly.*

# Chapter VII

Working in the hospital day in and day out gave Amara time alone with her thoughts. As mundane as laundry and dusting were, she cherished the quiet moments. She particularly enjoyed sweeping. Women had been doing that task since the beginning of civilization and when Amara was engaged in that activity, she felt a connection to her female ancestors.

Thinking of those women led Amara to reflect on her childhood friends. There were a couple of other little girls in her neighborhood growing up, but her mother preferred she associate with the daughters of fellow parish members. Get-togethers were few and far between and tended to be uncomfortable as the children barely knew each other and were constantly under their parent's supervision. Amara preferred to play with her brothers and their friends. They did fun things like play tag, cowboys and Indians, and rolled barrel hoops through the alleys.

While the boys went to school in a building a few blocks from their house, Amara was taught at home by her mother. When the Lucy Cobb Institute opened its doors on January 10, 1859, Amara's father insisted she be a part of the inaugural class. With an emphasis on gentle manners and old-fashioned accomplishments, he felt it would be the perfect environment to turn his puckish daughter into the belle she was meant to be.

At all of twelve years old, Amara was packed up and sent to the school which was to be her home for the next two-and-half years. The hours spent in the classroom were some of the happiest times of her life. A whole new world had opened up to her. She absorbed her lessons like a sponge—always eager to learn the newest material presented by her teachers.

Outside the classroom it was a different story. The girls who came from the well-to-do families taunted Amara to no end. They made fun of her unruly hair, the light freckles that dotted her nose and cheeks, the dresses hand-sewn by her mother. Once word got around about how well she did academically, she was mocked for being the teacher's pet.

The one place of refuge for her was the library. Amara escaped to that peaceful room whenever she could. Hour after hour she immersed herself in reading. Within a year, she had read every book of interest to her lining the dusty shelves so she began reading them all over again.

It was in the library that she finally made a true friend at school. Miss Brigid McGinnis shared not only Irish Catholic roots with Amara but her love for reading as well.

Brigid was fortunate enough to come from money but wasn't like the other girls with their pert little noses sticking up in the air. She was kind and generous and never talked ill of anyone. Amara always thought Brigid's parents had aptly christened her, as she was the closest person to a saint Amara could think of. With her chestnut-colored hair, emerald eyes and tiny build, all she needed was a halo painted above her head to complete the saintly look.

When Amara came back to school in the fall of 1860 after her mother passed away, Brigid was there to comfort her and encourage her to refocus on her studies. She convinced Amara that staying busy would take her mind off of things and keeping her grades up would make her mother proud.

The advice worked, as Amara once again went to the head of her class. Little did she know that would be her last year of formal education.

When Amara and Brigid parted ways on the final day of

school in May of 1861, they anticipated seeing each other in the fall. However, that summer, when the obligatory twelve months of mourning were complete, Joseph McKirnan remarried. As Theresa had not been formally schooled, Mr. McKirnan felt it was his duty to send her to the Lucy Cobb Institute. Times being what they were, he couldn't afford to send two girls there, so his own daughter was obliged to relinquish her spot. Amara and Brigid corresponded for several months, but as the conflict continued, the mail service was less dependable and eventually the letters to each other trickled to an end.

Amara stopped in mid-sweep, put both hands on top of the broom and rested her cheek on her hands.

"Saint Brigid, if you're listening, watch over your namesake, my dear friend. Please ask God to keep her and her family safe."

Letting out a sigh, Amara resumed her sweeping, wishing her cares could be swept away as easily as the dust dancing at her feet.

# Chapter VIII

Nathan had cause to say his prayers at that moment as well. The train was within ten miles of its final destination. *If only we were a handful of miles from Texas*, he thought dejectedly. He missed his ranch and the friends he left behind more than he would have imagined. All that work he and Dominic had done to get it up and going may be for naught. A wry smile came to his lips as he thought about it.

*1859*
*That first summer on the ranch it didn't take long for him and Dominic to settle into a daily routine. A garden was planted to supplement their food supplies. Animals were cared for, chores completed. A trek into town garnered news about the local area, and occasionally national and international reports as well.*

*Herding the cattle to their land had been a chore, but nothing compared to the backbreaking work of branding each animal. However, with no fences, the markings were the only way for the men to ensure their property remained in their own hands. Dominic had the unenviable job of securing the steer close to the fire while Nathan heated up the branding iron with its distinct ND marking and applied the iron to each animal's backside. Once the metal hit its mark, the steer inevitably bolted, sometimes taking Dominic along for the ride.*

*As the days turned into weeks and the weeks into months, Nathan and Dominic kept to themselves, feeling no need to advertise the fact that they were Northerners and be labeled Unionists. Negroes comprised a third of the population of the state and slave labor kept ranches* and farms thriving. Nathan was against slavery but his neighbors embraced it. With a distorted sense of morality, the locals justified the practice, citing a biblical precedence on the issue.

The two young men worked sunup to sundown. In the evenings, Nathan sketched out house plans by lamplight. It made sense to use construction methods that were compatible with the climate of the region. A two-story dog trot structure facing south would provide superior ventilation, thus keeping the interior temperature moderate even on the hottest of days. Cedar timbers from neighboring wooded lands could be hauled in by wagon. He planned to construct a separate kitchen and smokehouse to keep the main dwelling cooler and reduce the risk of fire.

With materials in hand, Nathan and Dominic began construction of their house. They made steady progress in the few hours they had to devote to the project each evening. A well needed to be dug before the weather turned cold. The river supplied drinking water but it would be more convenient to have a source close at hand. Coal stores on the property were augmented each time they headed into town.

As fall neared, the building was almost complete. The two made preparations for their first cattle drive, including finding someone to keep an eye on the ranch while they were gone. Most ranchers chose to drive south to port cities to ship their cattle out East. Nathan, however, reasoned that heading north on the Shawnee Trail towards markets in Missouri and Iowa made the most sense.

While the path led through Indian territory, ranchers were less wary of the Indians than they were of the farmers who attempted to obstruct passage through their lands. Some Longhorns carried a tick that infected the *indigenous cattle and local farmers did whatever was necessary to protect their own livestock.*

*Nearly half of Nathan's cattle were mature enough to be brought to market on the first drive. Determining that the quickest route from their ranch to their final destination in Kansas City, Missouri, was a straight line, they rode through Oklahoma Territory. No harm befell them, but once they crossed the Missouri state line, trouble loomed.*

*"Looks like we've got some company," yelled Dominic above the sound of the pounding hooves. Nathan had also seen the band of riders approaching and felt a sense of unease. Whistling to Checkers to slow the herd down, Nathan motioned Dominic to ride out with him to meet the armed men.*

*"Howdy, boys," drawled the lead rider as the group pulled up, surrounding Nathan and Dominic. "Looks like you two are driving yer cattle through our property. You know where you is right now?"*

*"If I've got my bearings straight, I'd say we're in the southern-most portion of Missouri, sir," replied Nathan, trying to size up his opponent while he considered options for getting out of this predicament.*

*"Right you are there, boy. Where you from and where you heading with them steer?"*

*"Northern Texas to Kansas City, sir," said Nathan as his horse moved under him skittishly, eyeing up the surrounding horses.*

*"Who gave youse permission to stampede across my property?" inquired the man, squinting as he looked at Nathan dead on. "I don't cotton to folks driving cattle cross my land uninvited. We're not keen on having our cattle infected by your lousy steers."*

*"Sir," interjected Dominic. "Each one of these steer was hand-picked on the auction block by my partner and me*

*and inspected snout to tail. They're clean and healthy."*

*The man didn't look impressed.*

*"But as a show of good faith," added Dominic hastily, "we'll give you one of them. If any of your cattle becomes infected on account of our steer, we'll pay you back for your loss when we pass through next."*

*The self-appointed leader drew his men aside to discuss the offer.*

*"Make that two steer and you's got yourself a deal," said the man, approaching Dominic on his horse. "But we knows yer mark and if'n you cross us, you'll regret the day you ever stepped foot on this here piece of ground."*

*"Yes, sir."*

*Two steer were roped and led off with the group and they galloped away, leaving a cloud of dust in their wake.*

*"Nice, Dominic," said Nathan with admiration.*

*"Let's just hope we don't have to give away two animals every time we're waylaid, or we might have a lean herd to sell at auction," Dominic replied as he took his hat off and wiped a dusty sleeve across his forehead.*

*The duo made their destination with no further occurrences. They managed to triple their investment in the animals at the market, while still maintaining a core group of breeding stock at the ranch. The profit was put back into their business to expand their operation.*

*The winter of 1860 was cold, but the cedar walls proved to be sturdy and kept the elements at bay. The herd grew when calfing started in the spring. Fields were tilled for grain production. The pair took on several hired workers, including a woman to tend the house and do the cooking.*

*Life on the ranch was fulfilling for Nathan. Each day he woke up with the sun, eager to face the challenges set before him. He relished the smell of the land, the simple beauty of the plains, the gentle rhythm of life's cycles.*

*There may not have been a church within a day's ride of his homestead, but he certainly felt God's presence. He maintained his ritual of going to Mass in his mind each evening while he envisioned the church they would construct on their property someday. All it would take was verification from the Diocese of Galveston that a saddle priest would be available to lead their small flock.*

*There's just one thing missing in my life, Nathan thought as he sat on his porch watching the sunset one evening. Tipping back in his chair with his feet propped on the porch railing, he visualized a woman by his side, children running and laughing at their feet.*

*The thought faded as more troubling considerations entered his mind. Northern Texas was becoming a hornet's nest as abolitionists and secessionists clashed more frequently. Governor Sam Houston was vehemently opposed to secession but politicians were clamoring for it.*

*Spring turned into summer. As the heat rose, tempers rose as well. The Texas Troubles, as they came to be known, broke out after a series of fires nearly destroyed the city of Dallas on July 8. Temperatures reaching 110 degrees that day were the probable cause, however many Texans blamed the fire on abolitionist preachers and Negroes bent on destroying northern Texas in retaliation for the whipping of two abolitionist Methodist ministers the previous year.*

*Nationally, the Democratic Party was split between Stephen Douglas, a Northern Democrat, and John Breckinridge, a Southern Democrat. This led to the stunning presidential victory by Republican Abraham Lincoln on November 6, 1860. In Nathan's mind, Lincoln could very well be the man who could veer the United States away from conflict. Within weeks, though, South Carolina seceded from the Union.*

*By the end of January 1861, Mississippi, Florida,*

*Alabama, Georgia and Louisiana followed suit. The question of secession was posed to the residents of Texas, which had entered the Union as a slave state in 1845. Nathan and Dominic were in the minority of voters. By a margin of three to one, on February 1, 1861, Texas became the seventh state to secede.*

*While the country teetered on the edge of all-out hostilities, Nathan and Dominic continued operating their ranch. Everything changed on one spring day that would forever be branded in Nathan's mind. He and Dominic had been working side by side constructing a chicken coop. When they saw a horseman coming towards them at breakneck speed, they looked at each other in apprehension. Nathan's heart sank as the rider pulled up to them, relayed a brief message, and then continued on his frenetic journey. Regardless of all the talk, the newspaper reports, the blustering and bellowing on both sides of the issue, Nathan could not believe it had come to this. "Holy God, what have we gotten ourselves into," he said under his breath, tilting his head skyward.*

*As of April 12, 1861, the nation was at war.*

# Chapter IX

It looked like the train ride was going to be extended for a bit for Nathan and his fellow soldiers. The vehicle slowed down until it was at a complete standstill. A wayward bull had somehow meandered onto the tracks and wasn't all that keen about vacating his position. Yelling and cussing the beast out didn't appear to bother it one iota. *Must be an Army bull*, Nathan thought to himself with amusement.

It would take a little more prodding than that, so the men in the engine were drawing straws to see who would have the honor of running the animal off the track. The pause gave Nathan more time to think back on the start of the war and how he became enmeshed in it.

*1861*

*News of battles raging throughout the southern and eastern states had reached Heavenly Vista Ranch sporadically the first year of the hostilities, but Nathan and Dominic concentrated on the business of running their place. While other ranchers gathering at the grange spewed on about states' rights and showing Mr. Lincoln what the South was really made of, the two young ranchers kept mute on the topic.*

"Simmons, y'all been in these parts for a while now," noted a lanky, sun-beaten cowboy one day as Nathan was in town picking up supplies.

"Yes, sir, I'd say I have."

"Then y'all know we Texans, we're a proud bunch. We didn't kick Santa Anna's rear end back to Mexico just so we could be pushed around by some other fella bent on meddlin' in our affairs."

"No, sir."

"Boy, why ain't you taken up arms with Lee's Army yet? They's looking for young bucks like you to show them Yanks what's what."

"Sir, I'm supporting Lee by providing meat to feed his troops. I might be able to shoot down a couple of Yankees, but I can feed hundreds of our boys with this beef. I figured that makes more sense."

"Guessin' you's got a point there. But if the Feds comes a-knockin' on your door, you's best be ready to defend the Lone Star state."

"I will, sir," said Nathan, hoping his face portrayed the conviction he was sorely lacking.

The battle that was to be fought and won within weeks looked to be turning into a full-out war. The fighting got no closer to Nathan's ranch than two spots along the Gulf of Mexico in the far southern reaches of the state. Navy personnel clashed on Sabine Pass in the fall of 1862 and 1863. Galveston was the spot of a confrontation but no casualties in October 1862. On New Year's Day 1863, the Confederates bested the Union forces on the water, securing Galveston Harbor's position as one of the last lifelines for the Confederacy to the outside world.

Nathan and Dominic managed to herd their longhorns north in the fall of 1862 and 1863, but were now joined by scores of other ranchers. With the turmoil along the gulf, it was risky driving the cattle to the major ports. As the northern route became more firmly established and as more farmers left to join the service, the men were able to pass without incidence.

The war came to Nathan and Dominic's doorstep in the spring of 1864 when a company of men rode up to the ranch house one morning. Sharply dressed Confederate officers on horseback preceded a horse-drawn wagon holding a collection of men of varying ages.

*"Are you thinking what I'm thinking?" asked Dominic as he and Nathan emerged from the barn.*

*"I'm guessing they're not out for a hay ride," replied Nathan wryly.*

*"This your ranch?" questioned the captain from atop his mount.*

*"Yes, sir," said Nathan*

*"Any other men other than you two under the age of thirty-five living on this here property?*

*"No, sir,"*

*"Very well. By orders of Colonel Alfred Harris Abernathy, you men are hereby conscripted to the Army of the Confederate States of America. You have five minutes to gather your essentials and any firearms you might own."*

*By the look on the man's face, Nathan knew he wasn't going to take no for an answer. "Did you hear me," yelled the captain as he made motion to reach for the pistol at his side.*

*"Yes, sir," yelped back the men in unison.*

*Nathan and Dominic did an about-face and strode towards the house. Once inside, they rifled through their belongings, grabbed their pistols and met up in the hallway.*

*"You know I can't fight for the Confederate Army, Dominic," said Nathan in a low voice.*

*Dominic nodded in agreement.*

*"David has been fighting on the side of the Union since this whole thing began and Stephen joined up in January when he turned eighteen," Nathan continued. "There's no way in hell I'm going to put myself in a position where I could be firing at my own brothers."*

*"I hear you, Nathan," said Dominic. He looked at Nathan pointedly. "Are you thinking what I'm thinking?"*

*"If you think we need to escape from those thugs the*

minute their backs are turned, then the answer is yes. Ideally we'll be able to do this together but don't wait for me if you see an opportunity to flee. We can make our way back to the ranch and lay low until things simmer down. If the North keeps driving like they have been recently, this conflict could be settled within a few months."

Dominic nodded in consent. The two shook hands and then Nathan summoned Maria.

The cook appeared from the dining room, drying her wrinkled hands on the apron tied around her ample waist.

"Dominic and I are leaving the ranch."

A questioning look came to Maria's face.

"We've been 'invited' to join the Rebel Army," said Nathan with a bitter tone. "I need you to get word to the other men. This isn't an order but a request. I'd like them to keep this place running until we get back."

"Si, Señor," replied Maria, her brown eyes filled with concern.

"Maria, I would be grateful if you would stay on as well."

The woman nodded her head vigorously. "Si, Señor. I pray daily to Santa Maria for Señor Nathan and Señor Dominic." She made the Sign of the Cross and mumbled a brief entreaty in Spanish, looking heavenward.

"Bless you, Ma'am." Nathan grabbed Maria's shoulders and kissed her on either cheek before hurrying outside.

Nathan and Dominic joined the other recruits in the wagon. Nathan couldn't drag his eyes away from the ranch as they rolled away, trying to capture the image in his mind. The beautiful, cloudless blue sky, the grove of trees, the flowers dotting the landscape, the crops in the field, the barn and the house built with their own hands.

*Another journey, but God only knew where they would end up. A Bible passage came to Nathan's mind— Philippians 4:13. He hadn't thought of it in years. When he was a youngster and misbehaved, his mother would hand him the family Bible and make him meticulously copy verses onto his school slate. All these years later, his impeccable script and knowledge of the Bible attested to Nathan's penchant for getting into trouble.*

*"I can do all things through Christ which strengtheneth me," he whispered under his breath.*

*He just hoped to God that was true.*

\*\*\*

*Being herded from wagon to train to wagon again that last week of April, Nathan and Dominic felt empathy for what they put their longhorns through each year. Their initial destination was Memphis, where they connected with the 53rd Tennessee Infantry. The company had been decimated by a round of measles the previous winter and they were looking to rebuild their ranks.*

*As men were assigned to various companies, the two friends stood close to each other with the hope of being placed together. The plan worked as both were dispersed to Company H.*

*Over the course of the next few weeks, the recruits were drilled under the watchful eye of Captain Robert S. Walker. Neither Dominic nor Nathan had any experience with swords but they caught onto the art of fighting with them quickly enough. Nathan's skill with his pistol and natural leadership ability garnered the attention of his commanding officer. Before they saw any action, he was promoted from private to corporal.*

*The uniforms issued to the men were anything but uniform. The trousers and jackets were in various styles*

and shades ranging from gray to butternut. It was
difficult finding anything that wasn't bloodied or shot
through—it certainly made the men wonder about the
former occupants. Finding a pair of trousers the proper
length was a trick for Nathan, but he managed to secure
one after a squabble with a youth a head shorter than
himself.

As the prospect of battle grew nearer, Nathan was
waging a war within himself. In his mind, all the skills he
had diligently been developing would be put to use in due
time fighting for the Union. But he hadn't yet conjured a
way to slip from camp unnoticed. Even if he could get
away, it was still a matter of locating Major General
William T. Sherman's forces, which were rumored to be in
the vicinity. Even at that, the sentries on duty would be
likely to shoot first and ask questions later if they saw a
man dressed in gray strolling into their camp.

Pulling Dominic aside one evening, Nathan shared his
troubled thoughts with his friend in hushed tones.

"Dom, a battle is brewing. I can feel it in my bones."

"I'm sure of it myself," agreed Dominic. "All the hairs
on my arms are standing on end. We'll soon be getting
our first taste of war."

"Have you thought yet what you will do when we're in
the thick of it? It grieves me to think I may be fighting
against my kin."

Dominic considered that possibility before he said his
piece. "Nathan, this is war. It's either kill or be killed. If,
by some chance, we do find ourselves in that
circumstance, I figure we'll get our chance to make
amends with our loved ones when we meet in the great
beyond."

"Let's pray we won't be faced with that situation."
Nathan said a quick Our Father to himself before looking
over either shoulder to assure their continued privacy.

*Lowering his voice further, he broached the next subject. "This may be the chance we've been looking for. When the fighting starts, if you see an opportunity to sneak across the lines, take it. I'll do the same."*

*Offering his hand to Nathan, Dominic nodded in agreement. "God willing, we will meet back at the ranch someday. Stay safe."*

*"Stay safe yourself, Dom," said Nathan, shaking Dominic's hand firmly.*

*Within hours, orders were passed through the company that they would advance on Union forces gathered near Dallas, a speck on the map northwest of Atlanta.*

*It was ironic that Nathan faced his first battle in that particular locale. He longed to see his Dallas and all of Texas again. He missed the beauty of the open range, the wildflowers covering the land as far as the eye could see, the night sky with more stars than a man could count, and the endless plains he spent hours roaming with Isis.*

*When the troops were assembled, they began marching towards their destination. Tuesday, May 24, 1864, thought Nathan in cadence, committing the date to memory. I will tell my children and grandchildren about this someday—assuming I survive this fiasco.*

*The moment a bullet whizzed past Nathan's head and lodged into a tree behind him, all thoughts turned to the task at hand. A barrage of firing began and men scrambled for cover amongst the trees. Orders were shouted to advance.*

*What started out as shooting from a distance turned to hand-to-hand combat as the forces fell upon each other. Nathan blasted as many shots as he could, each one deadly accurate, before he had to abandon his firearm and grab his sword from its scabbard. Years of manual labor gave him the strength to fight on when many fell around him.*

As quickly as it started, the skirmish ended, with both sides retreating to regroup and collect their casualties. Nathan was one of the lucky ones, coming out virtually unscathed, save minor cuts and a sore jaw from a blow to the face. Dominic's fate was unknown. Nathan looked at each body being dragged off the field, but didn't spy his friend among the living or the dead. He inquired about Dominic with any man he came upon, but his search was in vain. *Please God, let this mean Dominic has escaped,* he prayed.

With the dawn of each new day, the guns were fired up and the fighting began anew. Nathan began to feel numb to the death and dismemberment surrounding him. His goal was to survive, one minute at a time, until either a victory was secured or they abandoned this hellhole altogether.

Luck stayed on Nathan's side as the battle waged on. By the sixth day, the Union forces were tiring of the game of cat and mouse. As the sun rose, an eerie silence fell over the field. Rather than the sound of small arms fire, the men in Nathan's unit heard the rumble of wheels.

"Holy sh..." was the last thing Nathan remembered hearing before a cannon projectile shot past him, decapitating the soldier who had been at his side. The entire company turned on their heels, running pell-mell through the trees. The next round was as deadly as the first and a score of men went down, including Nathan.

"God bless it," said Nathan, gritting his teeth as his shirt slowly turned from white to crimson. The blow had knocked him to his knees and he struggled to get up, knowing the Yanks were on his tail. He had a searing pain in his side but, glancing around him, he saw that most of the other soldiers had fared much worse than he had. Body parts were scattered throughout the area and dead men with holes blown through them seemed to gape *in disbelief at their fates. Grabbing a tree trunk, he pulled himself up and began to move. If I can just make it back to camp, I'll find help there, he thought as he lumbered forward, his head spinning.*

*His momentum picked up as he got closer to his destination. The camp was in view and men dragged in bodies, reloaded guns and ran for cover. Nathan blacked out within feet of the white canvas flap of the surgeon's tent.*

*When he awoke, he was lying face up on the ground, surrounded by other injured men. The surgeon looked him over with a weary countenance.*

*"Son, you've got a nice collection of grape shot in you. We're going to wrap you up and get you on the next train to Atlanta to have a surgeon clean you up."*

*Shaking his head to clear the cobwebs, Nathan looked the man in the eyes. "Any vital organs damaged?"*

*"I'd say not, son, otherwise we wouldn't be having this conversation, would we?"*

*"I'm not sure what they hit, but I'll tell you what, it hurts like hell."*

*"Not nearly as much as it would if I were to attempt to dig out the shot in the field. Our laudanum resources are depleted. There's not enough whiskey here to numb the pain of surgery."*

*"Do they have capable surgeons in the city, sir?"*

*"Young man, I'm sending you to Atlanta to the best surgeon I know. Doc Burgess will have you fit as a fiddle in no time."*

*To fight for the Rebel cause? Over my dead body, thought Nathan sarcastically. In his estimation, the South didn't have the munitions or the manpower to win a war. It wasn't worth risking his neck to keep fighting a losing battle. In that moment he made a vow that, when he was able-bodied again, he was going to get over to the Union side, come hell or high water. With that final thought, Nathan slipped back into a blissful state of unconsciousness, a look of fortitude creasing his brow.*

***

The lurching of the train to a full stop brought Nathan back to the present. Looking out the window, he saw the town name Dalton scribbled on a slab of wood nailed to a post. It was time to start planning his escape.

# Chapter X

Darkness was falling as Amara completed her chores for the day. After putting her cleaning supplies away, she found herself drawn to the large window that faced north. She put her hands on the windowsill and put her head through the open portal and breathed in the evening air.

It was really the first deep breath she had taken in the past twelve hours. The dampness was refreshing after such a warm day. As she stared out into the gathering darkness, she began her evening ritual of praying for the people closest to her. She started with her father, then her mother up in heaven, her brothers, Uncle William, Brigid, Father O'Reilly, the parishioners at church, her old schoolmates and teachers, their neighbors, the people of Atlanta and, if she was feeling particularly generous, Mrs. McKirnan and Theresa.

She prayed more fervently for the Confederate soldiers still out on the battlefront, the families they left behind, all the men she'd interacted with during the day, their commanding officers and, in particular, President Jefferson Davis. She implored God to help Mr. Lincoln come to his senses, and finally call a halt to this foolishness and let everyone get on with their lives.

The stars were starting to peek through the sable sky. Amara could make out a few constellations as the night deepened. Tonight she had a final prayer for one soldier in particular.

"God, send your angels to watch over Corporal Nathan Simmons. Keep him in the hollow of your hand..." She swallowed hard, feeling guilty asking one more thing of a God who must be terribly preoccupied with a war going on and such. "And if it be Thy will, bring Nathan back to me."

With that off of her chest, Amara made the Sign of the Cross and turned away from the window.

*** 

At that very moment, Nathan was in the process of disembarking from the train. He took his time so he could survey the surroundings beyond the crowd on the platform. As the conveyance chugged away, the commanders were trying to make themselves heard over the rabble so they could gather up their various companies.

"53rd Infantry, Company H." Nathan recognized the voice of Sergeant Samuel Osborne, his commanding officer. What he lacked in stature, he made up for in volume. Nathan immediately hustled over to the edge of the woods where Osborne stood on a tree stump. He knew the man didn't take kindly to sluggishness.

Unfortunately, the recently inducted privates didn't know that.

Osborne bounded off the stump.

"You boys in Company H?" snapped Osborne, stopping a group of young men in their tracks.

The three bobbed their heads in unison.

"What was that?" he said in an irate tone.

"Yes, suh," squeaked out one of the lads.

"The mules on my pappy's farm walks faster than you. You boys mules?" asked the sergeant, poking his stubby pointer finger towards each man's chest to punctuate his words.

"No, suh," they stammered.

"I thinks you just may be. Seeings that's the case, we's gonna make youse the pack mules for this here company."

"Load up these young asses with the equipment we're hauling." Osborne directed the command to two corporals inventorying the supplies.

"Yes, suh," came the reply, accompanied by stiff salutes.

When the men were loaded up the group began marching the three-mile trek to their post. Threats of being donkey-whipped kept the young men moving at a brisk pace despite their heavy cargo.

Nathan felt sorry for the trio but dared not intercede. He didn't want the sergeant turning his attention on him. As they trudged along, gamely trying to stay in cadence despite the uneven terrain, Nathan formulated a plan that had germinated in his mind earlier that evening.

Since it appeared that Dominic had managed to escape, Nathan was on his own. From what he heard, the men in Company H were to be meeting up with the 53rd Tennessee Infantry soon. If he was going to make a break he wanted to do it before they moved.

One thing Nathan had noted on the train ride was that the new recruits—pups straight off their daddies' farms—were dressed in civilian clothing. Considering the sorry lot of uniforms he had to choose from months earlier, he couldn't imagine they had much of anything left for these greenhorns. That may just play into his plans. Securing different clothing was imperative—he just needed to figure out how to do that without causing an uproar.

With the first portion of his plan somewhat sketched out, Nathan considered his destination once he left the encampment. While he was laid up at the hospital, news had trickled in from the warfront. Lieutenant General John Bell Hood and Lieutenant General William J. Hardee were holding onto Dalton for the Confederacy. Union forces led by Major General John M. Schofield and Major General James B. McPherson held positions north and west of the city respectively.

Nathan had always thought that if he managed to escape the confines of the Rebel Army, he would make his way back to his ranch. Yet, as much as he yearned to put the war behind him, Nathan felt compelled to join the

Union forces. He could use the skills and knowledge acquired over the last several months to fight for his country. The ranch was in capable hands. Maria's husband Eduardo, the free black Ol' Joe, and the Cherokee elder Saligugi—Snapping Turtle to the white man, could outwork men half their ages. There weren't any cattle left so the three of them should be able to take care of the remaining livestock and the crops so the ranch could stay in operation.

Nathan had hastily scribbled a will on that fateful day when he was led away from the ranch. In the event of his demise, Dominic would own the property. If neither of them survived, the land would be turned over to his younger brothers. Maria acted as witness, scratching her X on the bottom of the page.

Making his way south back towards Atlanta seemed like the prudent choice. Finding a Union camp shouldn't be a difficult task, but walking in without getting shot may not be as easy. Wearing civilian clothes could give him valuable seconds to pitch his story to the sentry on guard. Whether the soldier would believe him or not was a different matter. *I'll cross that bridge when I come to it.*

As Nathan and the rest of the troop came upon the camp, the sergeant halted the men as he acknowledged the guard. In that moment, Nathan spied his mark. A lanky new recruit, a good head taller than his friends, stumbled in behind the rest of the men. *He's a gullible looking fellow if I've ever seen one,* considered Nathan.

Tents were pitched throughout the clearing and blazing fires were encircled by men seated on the ground or lounging against trees. Kettles of stew cooked over the open flames, the aroma hitting Nathan and making him realize how hungry he was.

"Get yerself some chow, then find a spot to rest yer lousy heads tonight," commanded the sergeant.

Nathan gave the officer a wide berth as he walked into the camp.

"Squirrel stew? Can't hardly believe there'd be any four-legged critters left in these woods," said Nathan as he approached a group of men he recognized.

Jumping up, his fellow corporal, Robert Petty, threw his arms around Nathan in a bear hug, nearly lifting him off the ground. "Speaking of critters, you're one I never thought I'd see again," he said as he released him. "Fellows, looks like Simmons has about as many lives as an ol' Tom cat."

The other men greeted him more formally but looked happy to see him nonetheless. *A person can't help but like this guy*, thought Nathan as he looked at his burly comrade. A pang of guilt hit him as he realized in the near future he could very well be trying to kill him and these other men he had come to know as well. *Civil war?* That's an oxymoron if he ever heard one.

The group invited Nathan to join them and as they ate their stew Nathan related his tale of being injured and recuperating in Atlanta. The soldiers gave him firsthand reports of the fighting they'd encountered, and the comrades they had lost since they'd last seen each other.

By the end of their conversation, the camp was starting to settle down for the evening. Men shuffled off to their tents and Nathan's group disbanded as well.

"We should probably hit the hay," said Robert, yawning widely. "Simmons, you can bunk with me and these other three fellas here if it suits you."

"Sounds good, Rob. Just give me a couple minutes. I'll put out the fire."

"Take your time, buddy. If you's a prayin' man, put in a good word for me. All hell's goin' to break loose in the next two, three days."

"Will do," said Nathan solemnly.

Once Robert took his leave, Nathan looked over the camp, noting where the guards were posted. He could feel his heart racing as he contemplated his plan and the consequences if things didn't go well, the most severe being loss of life—his namely. But fighting on the side of the Rebels seemed like a death sentence with the tide of the war turning. In his mind, if he managed to make it in one piece to the Union lines, his chances of surviving this war would increase exponentially.

He watched the new recruits as they were assigned sleeping arrangements, and Nathan knew the tent that housed his man. Looking up at the moon through the cloudless sky, he weighed his options for escaping. As much as he wanted to leave immediately, he would need cloud cover to shroud his departure. He prayed clouds would come upon them before it was too late.

# Chapter XI

Saturday morning Amara decided to make a quick stop at the hospital to catch up on some minor tasks. Apparently there was a lull in the fighting around Atlanta as no new patients had been admitted over the past twenty-four hours. She spent her time organizing supplies, washing bandages and cleaning instruments. According to her uncle, forward thinkers in the medical community were suggesting that infectious diseases may be spread through the use of soiled medical equipment. That seemed logical to her, so Amara set about boiling water in large vats in the back kitchen to thoroughly cleanse each device.

She was thankful the hospital was silent when she left because she knew her father would never allow her to work the next day, as it was Sunday, the day the good Lord had instructed His faithful to rest. Finishing her tasks shortly after noon, Amara scampered to church for confession, hoping to arrive before her stepmother. The ever-pious woman would be sure to remind her stepdaughter of her shortcomings that she could relate to the priest. However, running short of sins to confess was the last thing Amara had to worry about considering the week she had just gone through.

The next morning, Amara dutifully attended Mass at Immaculate Conception Church with her family, but she had a hard time concentrating. The sun shone through the stained glass windows of the frame building, illuminating the family pews which seemed to be less full each week. The droning Latin caused her mind to wander and she pondered the fate of the young men in their parish community. Her thoughts then turned to the Texas corporal. *He's probably met up with his company by now,* thought Amara as the familiar strains of Ave Maria sprang forth from the organ and the male voices in the choir took up the song. *It's been calm around here; hopefully it's calm wherever his company is now as well.*

As if he could feel her disquiet, Amara's father put his arm around her shoulders as the song came to an end. *Ave Maria—one of Mother's favorite hymns. Does Father miss her as much as I do?* She looked up at him and catching his attention, gave him a smile. He gave her shoulder a brief squeeze and smiled back.

Father O'Reilly didn't seem to notice the oppressive heat in the church as he preached for all he was worth. His voice was uncharacteristically deep for a man of his stature—he was barely as tall as Amara and had a slight build. The ebony hair crowning his head, fair skin and blue eyes revealed his heritage as much as his brogue.

*He's preparing all of us sinners for the fire and brimstone that lies ahead of us,* surmised Amara ruefully. *What was that he mentioned? Something about it being easier to put a camel through the eye of a needle than for a rich man to get into the kingdom of heaven? Or any man for that matter.* As if the list of mortal sins wasn't sufficient enough, the inventory of venial sins seemed to be endless. *It was enough to keep a saint wondering if he were worthy of admittance to the Promised Land.* Her mind wandered further afield as she thought once again about the Texan. *Was daydreaming during church about a man who looked like a god considered a sin?*

The requisite twenty-minute sermon continued and Amara's train of thought veered off again. She imagined herself in the arms of a tall, dark man waltzing around the gleaming floor of her uncle's ballroom as the strains of "Crown Him with Many Crowns" floated to their ears.

She could hear every chord and the sound reverberated

through her chest as the notes poured forth from an organ. *"Crown Him with Many Crowns?" That's an odd song to be dancing to.* Realization yanked her into complete consciousness. She sat up straight. *Was I lost in reverie the entire sermon?* Amara looked around guiltily. Sure enough, congregants were beginning to rise—except for James. A sharp nudge from her elbow brought him to attention and he reached for his crutches.

"I hope you know you just woke me from the best sleep I've had in a week, Sis," whispered James irritably.

"If Mrs. McKirnan corners you after church and asks what the sermon was about, don't come looking to me for answers," replied Amara as quietly as she could. *Not that I would know myself,* she thought sheepishly.

When Mass finally ended, Amara restrained herself from pushing her way through the crowd to get outside for some fresh air. She obediently stood in line with her father and stepmother as they greeted the priest and then went to chat with friends and neighbors. Amara itched to get home. Not only was she anxious to get out of her Sunday best—the starched collar, corset and layers of petticoats were enough to drive her up a tree—but Uncle William had loaned her some of his medical textbooks. She was curious to learn more about medical practices and human anatomy. Who knew, maybe she could be of further help to him somewhere down the road.

Her stepmother would be horrified if she could read Amara's thoughts. She wasn't keen on Amara helping out at the hospital in the first place. Proper young ladies assisted the war effort by knitting socks and praying to God for a swift Confederate victory. There was a reason only old and homely women were accepted as nurses, Mrs. McKirnan mentioned on more than one occasion. "But in due time that may be an acceptable position for you, Amara."

The barb didn't escape her.

Propriety be damned, she wasn't going to be sweeping floors if she could be helping Uncle William save lives. She would devour those textbooks cover to cover—just see if Mrs. McKirnan could stop her.

# Chapter XII

After two clear nights in a row, on Sunday, luck was finally on Nathan's side. The day started overcast with a slight drizzle and, although the precipitation stopped, the clouds never dissipated. Time crept slowly by as Nathan waited for nightfall. When the light in the sky was finally extinguished, he kicked dirt over the campfire, said a quick Our Father and then strolled to the targeted enlisted men's enclosure. He put on the airs of a man who didn't have a care in the world as he approached the tent.

A lively discussion filtered through the canvas as the four occupants inside talked about the girls they planned on courting when they got back home, knowing how the ladies loved to see a man in uniform. Nathan paused, listening for a moment. *War certainly seems exciting and romantic when you haven't been through it.* The other tents were quiet as the seasoned combatants readied themselves for the probable encounter with the Union Army on the morrow. From what Nathan had experienced, that entailed preparing a personal battle plan and making amends with the Lord—when any given day could be your last, there was no point in taking chances.

Quietly pulling back the flap, Nathan peered inside the dim area and took a moment to let his eyes adjust to the lack of light. The man he searched for was easy enough to spot as his feet nearly hung out the entryway.

"Good evening, men."

"'Evening, Corporal," said the men, spotting the insignia on his shoulder. They hastily struggled to sit up and salute the officer.

"No need to rise on my account. Just stopping by to make my acquaintance with the new folks in the neighborhood," said Nathan, surveying the group. "We've got ourselves a nice, calm night here. But word's out we might see some action in the morning."

"Action? You means fightin', suh?" asked the young man furthest from Nathan.

"That's exactly what I mean, Private. 'Course, before we set you boys out in the field, we need to get everyone in uniform.

The young men looked at each other in surprise. "I just knew we was gonna' get duded up," said a redhead, his face flushed with excitement. "And you says there ain't any more duds to be issued, Charlie. Guess I won that bet!"

"I guess you did," said Nathan affably. "So, let's do this one uniform at a time. We'll start with the tallest first. What's your name, son?"

"Andy Richardson, sir. Private Andrew Richardson."

"Follow me, Private Richardson. You other boys wait here, I'll be back for you shortly," said Nathan, tipping his hat. He held the flap open to allow the private to surface from the tent.

Nathan pivoted around and strode towards the edge of the camp in the direction where the necessaries had been dug. The private trotted behind at his heels. Because of the stench, the area was relatively deserted except for a young man hurriedly making his way back to camp.

"Sorry about the aroma, son, but the uniform stores are just beyond this area." Stopping in a grove of trees some thirty feet further, Nathan eyed the man up. "Since you're about my size, I'm going to have you try on my uniform to see if it's a proper fit. We'll swap clothes for a few minutes while I get your trousers and coat. Mind me, you're not allowed to follow me as the supply storage is off limits for men at your rank."

"Yes, suh," said Andrew, a look of dismay crossing his face. "Um, suh, I don't mean to question no orders or nothin', but I'm not so sure you'd be wanting me to put yer things on." Even with the limited lighting, Nathan could see the man's cheeks turning red beneath his peach fuzz. "Um, I ain't got no undergarments."

"Then we'll have to issue you some of them too, now won't we," said Nathan, trying to keep a straight face. "Let's do this quickly, shall we? There's more men waiting in line."

Andrew exchanged his shirt and trousers for Nathan's. After buckling his gun belt back on Nathan handed over his jacket and perched the slouch hat on the man's head.

"Why, don't you just make one fine soldier," said Nathan admiringly. "Your mama would be as a proud as a peacock if she could see you now. After you win this battle, you'll have to fight off the girls back home."

Andrew straightened his shoulders and cocked his head to one side. "Ya think so, suh?"

"Absolutely." Giving the young man a quick perusal, Nathan added, "Looks like we got ourselves a perfect fit. You just sit yourself down on that log. I'll be back in two shakes of a lamb's tail with your gear."

"Yes, suh. Thank you, suh."

Nathan saluted the soldier and walked deeper into the woods. Once he was out of Andrew's line of vision, Nathan began to run. He didn't exactly know where he was going but his intention was to head south.

He ran for a good forty minutes, slowing down only to catch his breath every so often. At one point he stopped, put his hands on his knees and started sucking air deep into his lungs. The faint smell of burning wood wafted into his nostrils. Nathan froze and concentrated on quieting his breathing and slowing his heart rate down so he could lessen the pounding in his cranium. Hearing nothing but the sounds of the nighttime inhabitants of the forest, he slipped behind a tree and leaned against the mossy bark for a few moments. *Lord, let this be a Union camp,* he prayed. Saying the Our Father and a Hail Mary for good measure, he made the Sign of the Cross, left his cover and inched his way closer to the scent of the fire and soon the sounds of an encampment. He stayed concealed behind the foliage, gently brushing leaves aside to get a better view. Ahead of him he could make out the shape of a flag, hoisted on a staff planted next to a dying fire. *Red and white stripes and thirty-five stars.* A sense of relief flooded over him. *Thank you, Lord.*

Nathan sank to the ground. He wanted to have a clear head before he advanced any further. What he needed most was some rest. Pine needles under a tree he had passed a ways back beckoned his weary bones. He crept to the spot and settled himself in. Exhaustion overtook him as he formulated the next step in his plan.

Awaking shortly after sunrise, Nathan started towards the camp. Pulling himself up to his full height, he stepped out from the copse of trees, put his hands in the air and said in the thickest Massachusetts accent he could muster, "Corporal Nathan Simmons, U.S. Army, reporting for duty."

# Chapter XIII

Monday dawned hazy and warm and the hospital was nearly empty of patients. It was probably just as well because Amara wasn't sure what good company she would be to anyone as she couldn't stop yawning. She had been up half the night reading. Theresa had gone to a friend's house after Mass and got permission from Mrs. McKirnan to stay overnight. That gave Amara the perfect opportunity to peruse the medical books at length. If Theresa had seen the manuals, without a doubt, she would have tattled immediately.

After studying the volumes, Amara was more determined than ever to be by her uncle's side in surgery when the next batch of casualties arrived. The human body was quite fascinating with its organs and systems. To be able to save a life by removing a bullet or setting a broken bone would surely be a gratifying experience.

Amara did a nominal cleaning of the ballroom and when she was done she sought out the doctor to broach the subject with him.

She found him in his office, poring over a stack of paper.

"Uncle Wil...I mean, Doc, may I have a moment of your time?"

"Certainly Amara," said the physician, rising from his chair. "Here, let's move those papers off the settee so you can take a seat there." William proceeded to stack the documents precariously on one of the many piles already littering the floor.

"What can I do for you, my girl?"

"Sir, first of all, I want to thank you for giving me the

opportunity to help out here. I'm glad I can be of service to you and our troops in some way."

"It's been my pleasure, Amara. You've been a bright spot in the lives of the many soldiers who convalesced here since you've joined us. I should be thanking you."

A smile lit Amara's face. "You're too kind, sir. I appreciate your generous praise."

She hesitated, took a deep breath and then proceeded. "To be honest with you, sir, I would like to do more. I believe I could help in a more meaningful way if you would allow me to."

"Hmm," contemplated Doc, stroking his chin as he commonly did when considering something. "You can read and write, which is more than I can say for most of the hired help around here. Perhaps you could help me organize this office and work on documentation procedures. It seems to be a never-ending chore. If this damnable war doesn't kill me, the paperwork will. Would that suit you, dear?"

"I would be happy to assist you with that process, sir. But may I be so bold as to take this one step further?" Amara asked hesitantly.

"And that would be...?"

Amara gathered her courage, tucked her hair behind her ears and blurted out. "I would like to assist you in the surgical ward."

Doc's eyes widened and his eyebrows arched over his spectacles. "Really now." He pulled his glasses down lower on his nose and looked at her over the top edge. "When I loaned you my medical books, the intent was to dissuade you from any thoughts of delving deeper into the medical field, not entice you to pursue it. What makes you think you want to do this?"

"Sir, I've looked them over cover to cover. The information fascinates me. I pick up things quickly. If I could train with you I am convinced I could help. Something tells me that this war is far from over. I believe things will get worse before they get better."

"Hmm," said Doc, nodding his head. "I'll tell you what. How about a taste of doctoring to see how it appeals to you? I assume the good ladies at Lucy Cobb Institute taught you how to apply needle and thread?"

"Yes, sir. I always scored admirable marks in stitching."

"Perfect. We have a soldier upstairs with a leg wound that needs restitching. Let us put your talents to use on his skin and see how well you do."

Amara had some reservations, but nodded in agreement and followed her uncle as he vacated the office and ascended the stairs to the second floor.

"Hello," Amara said cheerily as she approached the cot her uncle pointed out. The lack of insignia on the sack coat resting near the soldier's head indicated his rank. "Private, Doc tells me you have some handiwork that needs to be done on your leg. I'm here to close that wound properly."

"No offense, Miss, but you're a girl. You ain't no doctor," said the young man looking past Amara to Doc for affirmation.

"I'm well aware that I'm a female, but I'm also Doc's assistant today. Now, let's take a peek. Which leg is it?"

The man reluctantly pointed to his left leg." Amara pulled up the sheet covering the soldier's lower half, careful to keep his dignity intact.

She had to swallow hard as she took her first look at the injury. His thigh was sliced horizontally just below the groin area and the gaping cavity was swollen and oozing pus. The smell of rotting flesh made Amara's eyes water. The bile rose in her throat as she bent down to get a closer look. It was a clean cut, most likely from a saber, but it was a deep one, perhaps all the way to the bone. The gap between the two edges was a good three-quarters of an inch, so Amara wasn't sure she had strong enough filament to close the wound. That apparently had been the issue during the first attempt as bits of thread littered both edges of the opening.

Amara questioned her good judgment as she waited for the wave of nausea to pass. "Jesus, Mary, Joseph," she intoned under her breath.

"Private, if you want to keep that leg, it's going to need repair sooner rather than later," she said forcefully, looking into his frightened eyes, doing her best to sound braver than she felt. "You do want to keep your leg, don't you?" asked Amara, nodding her head.

The man nodded back in assent.

"Doc? Do we have anything to help ease this process a bit?"

Doc reached inside his coat and produced a flask of whiskey.

Amara eyed it up. "Is that for him or me?"

"Him now, you later, I'm guessing," said Doc with a wink. "We're saving the laudanum for the more desperate cases. Give him a swig and then bathe the wound with the alcohol to wash it out."

The soldier gladly accepted the drink and a bite-marked chunk of wood to clamp his jaws on before the process began. When Amara gingerly poured a dab of whiskey on wound, the man ground his teeth into the wood to muffle his scream and tears pooled in his brown eyes. Blinking back her own tears, she gave him a few seconds to muster his courage then proceeded to finish cleaning the area, pressing on the wound with a cloth to draw out the pus.

The doctor gave her a few instructions, then handed her a needle. Her fingers shook as she sterilized the tip of it in the candle flame. It took three tries to force the silk thread through the eye of the needle. She tied a double knot at the end and then turned back to the patient. He looked to be on the verge of passing out, which may be the best thing for him. The skin surrounding the gash felt hot to her touch. Looking closely at the aperture, she determined to come up on the furthest edge with the first stitch and work her way down. Doc assisted by pushing the edges of the wound together. Amara was taken aback when she applied the tip of the needle to the skin to make the first stitch. This wasn't like sewing fabric—it took considerably more force to push the needle through. Amara prayed the needle would stay intact until she finished her work.

After the first stitch was complete, she shot a sidelong glance at the patient. His head lolled to the side, so she knew he was unconscious. Not knowing how long he would stay out, she set her jaw and quickened her pace and started sewing neat, small stitches in earnest, willing herself to think she was mending anything other than human skin. When she finally completed the task, she doused the area with more whiskey and let the doctor inspect her work.

"Well done, young lady. You could have a career as a seamstress with stitches as fine as these."

"No, thank you," said Amara as she wiped the blood from her hands onto a cloth.

"Son," said Doc, "we're through." He grabbed the object from the man's mouth, wiping the saliva on his shirt sleeve. "You're a brave soldier. The stitches that young lady put in your leg will hold; you'll be back on your feet before you know it."

The man wasn't coherent, but a look of relief came to his face before he closed his eyes again.

"Excuse me, sir," interjected Amara. "I need to go wash up more thoroughly."

Amara left the room at a steady pace, but when she got to the steps she raced down them, rounded the corner to the kitchen, flew out the back of the house and proceeded to purge the entire contents of her stomach into the shrubbery. When she finally stopped heaving, Amara quietly let herself back into the house to find the nearest wash basin.

"It will get easier with time, my dear," noted Doc as he walked past the doorway.

Amara could feel herself flush head to toe. She wanted to reply with something that made her look slightly less incompetent than she was currently feeling, but one look at his bloodied shirt and she was back out the door fertilizing the bushes again.

# Chapter XIV

Having a gun barrel jabbed into his chest wasn't exactly the warm welcome Nathan had hoped to receive when he walked into the camp. Looking into the eyes of the soldier on duty, the hairs on Nathan's arm stood at attention. *Good God, the Union's recruiting them as young as the Rebs now.* Lowering his eyes, he could see the gun wavering as the man held it with two hands, his body shaking like a blade of prairie grass on a blustery day. *It's either his first day on watch or they're not used to unexpected company.*

"May I speak with your commanding officer?" asked Nathan in a steady voice, hoping to calm the soldier down. "I've been separated from my unit." *No lie there.*

"J-J-Johnny, we got an intruder," said the young man, his voice croaking.

Another man came running through the brush. *Just my luck. The pup's twin brother. If these two are trigger happy, this is not going to go well,* thought Nathan, doing his best to look calmer than he felt.

Before he knew it more men came crashing to the edge of the woods, surrounding Nathan like beasts set to devour a wounded prey.

"Do we got a Reb cornered?" asked an older fellow.

"I can assure you sir, I am not a Rebel," said Nathan in a supercilious tone.

"You may talk all fancy like, but you sure ain't dressed like no Yank," the man replied, eyeing Nathan up.

"Make way. Move aside," an authoritative voice commanded from the crowd.

Immediately the men stood at attention and saluted the

gentleman in full dress uniform moving past them. He couldn't have been much older than Nathan but the epaulettes on the man's shoulders indicated he was a colonel in the United States Army.

"What have we here?"

"S-Sir, I caught this varmint sneaking into camp," said the sentry.

"What say you to that?" questioned the officer, motioning the guard back.

"Sir, I am a Massachusetts man born and raised," said Nathan respectfully, crisply executing a salute with his right hand before putting it back in the air to indicate he was surrendering. "I have extensive training in marksmanship and am an excellent horseman. I've come to offer my services to your company."

"Quite impressive I'm sure. Why you happen to be wandering through the woods of northern Georgia in civilian clothing should prove to be an interesting tale, I'm sure. We shall speak privately in my headquarters. Men..." the colonel nodded to his aides. Two soldiers relieved Nathan of his gun belt and patted him down in search of other weapons. Disarmed, he followed the retreating commander with the soldiers at his heels.

The wall tent they came to was nondescript on the outside but the interior was another matter altogether. A rope bed in the center of the space was flanked by a night stand and a bench holding a porcelain basin and pitcher. Maps were laid out on the desk which was situated along the back wall. The space was completed by a dining table topped with a starched white tablecloth formally set with bone china.

"We haven't been formally introduced. I am Colonel John T. Wilder, United States Army of the Cumberland. And you are?"

"Corporal Nathan Michael Edward Simmons, sir."

"Under whose command?"

"Colonel Abernathy."

"Are you referring to Colonel Alfred Abernathy of the Confederate Forces?" queried the officer with a suspicious look on his face.

"Precisely, sir. But before you jump to any conclusions, may I be allowed to state my case?"

"You have thirty seconds," said the man, pulling out his pocket watch. "This story had better be good or your rear end will be hauled off to the stockade before you can whistle one note of Dixie."

Nathan took a breath and hastily recounted his narrative to the skeptical colonel. "As I said before, I am a native of Massachusetts. In '59 I purchased ranching land in Texas with a partner. The war seemed far off to us in the northern reaches of the state until we were conscripted into the Confederate Army this past April. I fought with the 53rd Tennessee Infantry and was injured during the Battle of Dallas. After recuperating in Atlanta, I was shipped back north and found the first chance I could to escape."

"That's quite the saga," said Wilder, glancing at his watch before depositing it in his pocket. "Why should I believe you are an ally when you could very well be a Rebel spy?"

"Sir, I can't tell you what to believe but I swear on my mother's grave that every word I uttered is God's truth. My younger brothers are out there somewhere fighting on the Union side. I do not want to face either of them on the battlefield, sir."

Wilder wearily rubbed the goatee on his chin while he considered the case before him for a few moments. "These are trying times and we don't often have the leisure for studied decisions so I am going to have to go with my gut, God help me if I'm wrong. I am a man of my word and I shall trust you are as well. Welcome to the Federal Army of the United States, Sergeant Nathan Michael Edward Simmons."

Nathan's face registered his surprise.

"Thank you, sir," he said automatically, saluting the officer. "If I may beg your pardon, sir, but you did hear me say that my rank was corporal, did you not?"

"That I did, but anything the Rebs do, we'll outdo them. Hopefully their loss will be our gain," said the colonel.

"I will do my best to serve my country with honor and help secure the ultimate victory for the side of the Union," said Nathan, saluting again.

"See that you do. So, are you as good of a marksman and rider as you say you are?"

"Sir, on my ranch I live in the saddle. My pistol never leaves my side. I can hit a rattler dead between the eyes fifty yards out."

"That being the case, gather up your arms, find yourself some proper clothing and we'll try to set you up with a mount. I have to warn you, though, horses are a rare commodity out here. If there is a horse available, I place no guarantee on its condition."

"That's perfectly fine, sir, thank you."

Nathan saluted the commander one last time and turned to take his leave. The colonel walked him back through the door and explained the situation to the soldiers standing guard outside the tent. One of the men was assigned to show Nathan around the camp.

Nathan couldn't stop marveling at his good fortune. This was beyond anything he could have planned himself. He was honored by the promotion bestowed on him by the colonel and being assigned to a cavalry unit was more than he could have asked for. His thoughts turned to Isis. He could use a horse like her to ride into battle; she was such an intelligent and faithful mount but, for her sake, he was glad she was back at the ranch out of harm's way.

A supply clerk issued Nathan blue trousers, a shirt and a frock coat, all of which had seen better days but at least fit well enough. The fact that they had an actual supply of uniforms reinforced Nathan's belief that the war was favoring the North.

One of the camp followers was commissioned to hastily stitch the yellow-striped chevrons onto the sleeves of the coat. An eagle hat, belt and sword completed the ensemble.

The seamstress was the first female Nathan had laid eyes on since he left the train station in Atlanta. She led him away from his escort to the Sibley tent she shared with a few of the other women attached to the unit.

"You're a handsome one," said the woman admiringly as she adjusted the jacket on Nathan after they stepped inside the dimly lit enclosure. The girl brushed up against him as she fiddled with the buttons on his shirt. The low-cut dress she wore showcased her womanly assets.

Nathan tried to put some room between himself and the girl. She was a tempting morsel, no doubt, with her exposed bosom, painted cheeks and the smell of rose water wafting from the bare skin on her arms.

"You might be wanting to have these trousers taken in a bit," she added, hooking two fingers on the either side of his waistband. "If you like, you can slip them off and I'll take care of everything right now." She tilted her head back to gauge his interest with her saucy hazel eyes, an inviting smile on her face.

The innuendo wasn't lost on Nathan. *Was this some sort of test?* Morally, he knew he shouldn't cross that line, but they were all alone and, in the heat of the moment, the temptation was overwhelming. He closed his eyes to get his thoughts together as the woman walked around him to continue her inspection. In that moment, a vision of Amara came to him, a look on her face that wavered between admonishment and hurt. The guilt he felt even contemplating the woman's offer made him take a hasty step away from her.

"Thank you, Miss, but everything seems just fine," said Nathan politely, putting himself even further away from her. Other men may have turned down her proposition because of the risk of contracting syphilis or some other vermin from her, but it was highly unlikely they'd turn her down because of some woman who in all likelihood they'd never see again. *I will be the laughingstock of the Union Army if anyone finds out.*

"Well, aren't we the uppity one," the girl snipped. She grabbed the mending pile, spun around and walked away with a practiced wiggle to her hips, letting him know in no uncertain terms exactly what he was giving up.

Leaving the tent, Nathan strode over to the far side of the encampment to see if there were any real 'ladies' over there. He'd fare much better with a filly any day, they were much less complicated than the females of his species.

The horses and mules he came upon looked relatively well-fed compared to the scrawny beasts the Confederate officers rode. The stable boy pointed out two horses Nathan could choose from. The pitch black mare caught his eye. She looked as war-weary as everyone else around the camp but he could see some spirit in her eyes still.

"Does she have a name, son?"

"If she do, it done gone to the grave with her master, suh," said the lad matter-of-factly.

"Then I shall name her Kalona," said Nathan as he walked around her and evaluated her flank. Not too scarred considering what she had probably gone through when she lost her owner. "That's Cherokee for raven. It seems fitting." He stroked the horse's mane. "What do you think, Kalona, girl? Can you fly across the battlefields like your namesake?"

The horse nuzzled Nathan's hand and looked at him trustingly.

104 Amanda Lauer

"Let's see if we can both get out of this alive, shall we?"

She gave a feisty neigh, as if to take him up on his challenge.

Within hours, the company received orders to head towards Kennesaw Mountain.

When Kalona was saddled, Nathan settled atop her and fell into rank with the other mounted soldiers. With the goal of familiarizing himself with his new unit, Nathan scanned the group, searching for a person who might be open to talking with him. He steered away from the rambunctious young men who looked like they were raring for a fight.

A bespectacled gentleman, who managed to balance the reins of his horse in one hand while perusing a small book held in the other, caught Nathan's attention. He didn't recall seeing him earlier when he was accosted by the other soldiers. Hopefully the man missed the encounter and wouldn't have any reason to distrust him.

Nathan trotted up to the soldier, easing Kalona alongside the other horse.

"Excuse me, Corporal, may I have a word with you?"

"Certainly," said the man, finishing the paragraph he was reading before turning his attention to Nathan. "I mean, certainly, sir." The enlisted man knocked himself in the forehead as he attempted to salute without dropping his tome. "Pardon me, sir. I was engrossed in this story. I had no idea a superior officer was addressing me."

"At ease, Corporal. Pardon me if I startled you. I'm Sergeant Nathan Simmons, newly assigned to this unit."

"Corporal Timothy Demarest, sir."

"Corporal Demarest, have you been with Colonel Wilder long? I'm wondering what fighting this division has encountered."

"Sir, I've been riding alongside the good colonel since the Tullahoma Campaign, near unto a year ago now. That was when we appropriated the fine animal flesh we now call our own. The speed advantage we've gained has given us the nickname the Lightning Brigade," he confided proudly.

"Very impressive," said Nathan approvingly.

"We've another advantage, too," Demarest continued, patting the firearm at his side. "Colonel Wilder helped most of us secure the money to buy our own Spencer repeating rifles. The Rebs never knew what hit them when we seized Hoover's Gap."

Nathan had heard tales of the weapon from his Confederate contemporaries but had never laid eyes on one before. "I would imagine. Do continue."

"We were used as decoys during The Second Battle of Chattanooga. Got close enough so General Bragg could eyeball us up and know we were closing in on him. That gave the 18th Indiana Artillery enough time to set up across the Tennessee River and shell the snot out of Chattanooga. After about two weeks, the general abandoned the city and hot-footed his Army of Tennessee across the border into Georgia."

"Sounds like you've seen your share of fighting."

"It comes and goes. Since that time the Union 4th Division, XIV Army Corps has encountered a few skirmishes but nothing to write home about. Of course that could be about to change."

"How's that?"

"Word's out that the Rebs are dug in around Kennesaw Mountain. They aren't likely to give up without a fight. I guess we'll find out soon enough."

"Indeed we will," replied Nathan as he nudged his horse to move ahead. "Godspeed to you, soldier. Thank you for your time."

Before long, the soldiers were setting their positions to begin the assault. From the moment Nathan set foot on the field in his Union blues, he realized that war was war, regardless of what side he was fighting for. Like Dominic had said months earlier, it was either kill or be killed.

It didn't take long before the Reb soldiers engaged their Union counterparts. Hunched down on Kalona's back, Nathan's aim was deadly accurate as he methodically loaded, shot and reloaded. Without the advantage of a repeating revolver, he needed to make every shot count. He lost track of the number of men he hit. Kalona stood her ground, not even flinching when Nathan's gun kicked back each time it discharged.

When it became apparent that hand-to-hand fighting was inevitable, Nathan dismounted and grabbed Kalona's bridle.

"Listen, girl. This is no place for a lady. Head back to the camp and I will get back to you as soon as I can." He slapped her on the rump, causing her to gallop away.

When they were on top of the Confederate soldiers, most of the men in Nathan's troop switched from guns to the long-handled axes issued to them by Colonel Wilder. Nathan resorted to his sword and fought valiantly alongside the men in the newly-christened Hatchet Brigade. The fighting continued until the call was given to retreat. Attacking an enemy entrenched in a mountain proved to be futile.

As the unit withdrew, Nathan hung back, scouring the field for survivors. The Rebs were retreating as well, their victory cry dying through the air as they got further away. The ensuing quiet was eerie as he made his way around the corpses littering the area.

A slight noise caught Nathan's attention. *Can someone have survived this holocaust?* He slowly turned in a complete circle, trying to assess from where the sound emanated.

"Does someone out here need help?" Nathan inquired urgently, perusing the scene. Out of the corner of his eye, he spied a slight movement.

Nathan picked his way over numerous bodies to reach the soldier he had seen moving. He rolled the man over and saw blood seeping from a wound in his upper thigh. Without a moment's hesitation, Nathan instinctively yanked off his belt and secured it above the deep cut, pulling it closed as tightly as possible. The blood flow discoloring the gray trousers stopped almost instantaneously.

"Sir, I've put a tourniquet on your leg to stem the bleeding," said Nathan. "It looks like you have a nasty lesion there."

The man struggled to open his eyes, squinting from the midday sun. "Have I been captured," he asked, a look of confusion on his face.

"No, sir. Both sides are regrouping. They'll be coming to collect the casualties soon."

Nathan took a closer look at the injured man. While he was positive he had never seen the lieutenant before, the unique color of his eyes looked strangely familiar.

The man shook his head as if to clear his brain and looked straight at Nathan, his brow furrowed. "You've saved my life. Perhaps I'm confused from the blow I took to the head, but isn't it the job of Union soldiers to take Confederate lives, not spare them?"

"Sir, I am not a butcher. You are no threat to our side in your present condition. There is no reason for you to die on this field today. Enough have passed here as it is."

Voices barely audible from the south of their position alerted Nathan that the Confederate soldiers were en route to collect their dead and wounded.

"Your men are coming. You'll be back to camp in no time. I need to depart before they catch sight of me."

"I am eternally grateful for your help, sir," said the lieutenant, mustering up the energy to give a brief salute. "I only wish I had the means to repay your kindness."

"If you want to repay me, take care of yourself and get home to your family when the hostilities are over and done."

With that, Nathan scampered through the trees in the direction of the camp, gripping his pistol in one hand and holding up his trousers with the other. Maybe he should have taken that hussy up on her offer. *That's what I get for taking the high road. So help me, if I trip on these damnable trousers and end up shooting myself, that will be the last good deed I ever perform.*

Arriving safely at the camp, Nathan felt all eyes turn towards him and it wasn't because he was on the verge of losing his britches.

Apparently word had spread about his accomplishments on the battlefield. His contemporaries gathered around him, thumped him on the back and shook his hand. Each man was trying to outtalk the next as they rehashed their versions of the fight they'd just gone through and the bravery they'd witnessed among so many of their comrades.

At that moment, Nathan felt he truly became a part of the Union brotherhood.

# Chapter XV

Just as her uncle had predicted, the task of assisting in the surgical unit did get easier as the weeks went on. Doc openly admired Amara's abilities and tested her skills with more complicated cases as they came about.

With the temporary lull in the hostilities, Amara was able to gain headway in the office area as well. She organized files, dealt with the never-ending clutter, answered correspondence, and took care of whatever paperwork she could decipher.

The news reached them that one General William Tecumseh Sherman of the Union Army was making his towards Georgia, with his eye on Atlanta. A series of battles that came to be known as Marietta Operations began on the ninth of June. Casualties from areas Amara was barely aware of—Brushy Mountain, Mud Creek, Pine Hill and the like—began trickling in.

Less than two weeks later, Confederate Lieutenant General John B. Hood's ill-fated attack on Union forces cost the lives of nearly one thousand Rebel soldiers, triple the number lost by Major Generals John Schofield and Joseph Hooker. Injured men poured into Atlanta. Amara was thankful she had some experience in the surgical ward before the deluge began. The hospital was filled to overflowing—every cot and square inch of floor space was occupied.

Amara worked with her uncle and the other nurses eighteen hours straight that day, assessing injuries, handing off the dead to the orderlies, assisting in surgery. She stepped outdoors only long enough to tell James she wouldn't be coming home that evening. As much as it pained her to add another venial sin to her list, she asked him to tell Mrs. McKirnan that she was going to be staying overnight with an old school mate. She didn't want to saddle him with the lie, but he was a willing accomplice. He left with the promise to bring her a fresh change of clothing the next day.

The following Monday, the next wave of casualties hit. This time Sherman went head-to-head against General Joseph Johnston at Kennesaw Mountain. While the Confederates hailed it as a victory, another thousand Rebs fell.

It took most of the week to patch up the men shipped their way. Amara was beginning to feel numb to the chaos that was going on around her. The first time she saw a soldier begging Doc not to amputate his leg, she couldn't hold back the tears. Her hands covered her ears to block out the screaming as the saw cut through ligaments, tissue and bone. She had to remind herself that the procedure was done to save lives, not to destroy them, despite what the soldiers claimed.

Amara wore herself ragged trying to keep up the ruse at home that she was still performing mundane tasks at the hospital. She kept an extra dress and apron on hand so she could change out of her soiled clothing before heading home each evening.

A break in the action came and lasted nearly three weeks into July. The next assault was the most fearsome struggle Amara had heard of yet. Just three miles north of Atlanta at Peachtree Creek, six thousand-some men, the majority from the South, were maimed or killed in one day.

Having spent forty-eight hours straight at the hospital, Amara didn't have the time or energy to continue the subterfuge with her family. James sought her out and she told him she wasn't leaving until every last man had been cared for. He could tell Mrs. McKirnan whatever he liked, she was too tired to care.

An hour after she dismissed James, Amara could hear the sound of artillery fire close at hand. *Good God, is the city of Atlanta under siege?* Amara barely had time to say a brief Hail Mary before wiping her brow with her sleeve and proceeding to another patient. *What next?*

Wounded men arrived in droves. The sound of gunfire drew closer, yet the orderlies were forced to lay men in the yard surrounding the house. The people working indoors could barely make a path through the bodies strewn about.

An eerie silence fell over the city after that horrendous day of fighting. Within a week, the lists of the dead and missing were posted near the courthouse. Amara couldn't stop herself from heading towards the square as she left the hospital to catch some sleep. She looked over the shoulders of other concerned citizens who scanned the casualty lists. *Twelve thousand dead and wounded?* The number was nearly unfathomable. She scanned the list for Michael's name, his classmates, their neighbors, the men from church. Her heart sank every time she recognized a name—their faces appeared in her mind's eye and she grieved for the lives cut short.

She stepped away but stopped in mid-stride, and made her way back through the crowd to make one more sweep through the printed entries. Praise God, his name wasn't there. For today, the Texan still survived. A lump settled in the back of her throat as she turned away from the square.

Amara hadn't cried in weeks, but tears welled in her eyes as she walked back to her father's house. It was a mixture of relief, seeing some precious lives spared, and a deep, all-encompassing sorrow. *So many souls lost. For what purpose? Aren't we supposed to love our neighbors as ourselves?* Her heart sank lower as she considered the fate of her oldest brother. Any hope she had for his survival was dashed as she thought once again about all the names hastily written on the sheets nailed to the trees in the square. Maybe his name wasn't posted in Atlanta, but there were countless trees in countless squares in countless towns across the country. It could very well be written somewhere; how would she know?

One battle faded into the next as the summer waned. Ezra Church, Utoy Creek, Dalton, Lovejoy's Station, Jonesborough all became familiar names to Amara. But regardless of the setting, she knew every battle just brought more misery, more destruction and tore their nation further apart.

\*\*\*

Nathan had the opportunity to witness more devastation of lives and property that summer than he ever could have fathomed. The Union 4th Division was caught up in Sherman's march towards Atlanta. The enlisted soldiers weren't privy to the general's thoughts, so they could only guess what their commander intended to do once he secured his prize. But it was commonly known that he was an advocate of total war—he was determined to bring the South to its knees.

# Chapter XVI

The casualties from Jonesborough poured into the hospital for seventy-two hours straight. Sherman was intent on tying a noose around Atlanta's neck by cutting off the Macon & Western Railroad south of the city. The fighting had been fierce.

His tactic was successful. By the end of the second day, General John Bell Hood evacuated Atlanta. His troops were ordered to burn the warehouse district to keep Confederate supplies out of Union hands. Amara could see the flames from an upper window of the hospital where she paused long enough to assess the situation. She was looking to gather news to pass on to the soldiers in the ward.

Smoke and soot settled over the city after the fires were contained. The stench of the inferno clung to Amara's hair and clothing as she once again looked out the window towards the street.

It seemed that many of the citizens left in the city were set on fleeing that evening. Gathering what possessions they could carry or cart away, they were following the path of the retreating soldiers. In the little time she had to observe the scenario, Amara saw a neighbor escorting his family away and several members of her parish hastily executing their departure as well.

Amara had no intentions of leaving. As long as the hospital stood and there were men to be taken care of, she would stay put. She knew her father would refuse to evacuate as well. He had made it clear to her weeks ago that he fled one home already and had no intention to be a refugee ever again. Mrs. McKirnan and Theresa would do whatever her father did.

After her initial appraisal, Amara avoided looking out the windows the rest of the evening. She could do nothing about the world beyond her door, but she could help save lives if she focused on her duties at hand.

With the Confederate soldiers out of the city that evening, Doc thought it best to have Amara escorted home by two of the orderlies. The streets were nearly abandoned by the time her shift was over. She was safely deposited at her residence with no incidence.

As soon as she was in the door, she went straight to the room she shared with Theresa. She didn't even bother to remove her dress. She was dog tired and fell asleep within seconds of her head hitting the pillow.

A noise awoke Amara in what felt like just moments later. The clock on the mantle in the dining room chimed six times. She double counted in her head to be sure. *It cannot possibly be morning, I just shut my eyes.* She turned to the window to check, opening her eyes just a slit. The sun filtered through the mottled pane of glass, promising another warm day.

Amara didn't feel one bit rested. Every muscle in her body ached. The images of the previous night flashed before her eyes, causing her to bolt upright in the bed, her heart pounding fiercely. At first she thought it was a nightmare, but reality came rushing back to her. *I want to wake up and have my life back to normal.* Amara slowly made her way from the bed, careful not to disturb Theresa who slept soundly as usual. It was hard not to be resentful looking at her, lost in her dreams with nary a care in the world to crease her brow. *Have you noticed that our country is falling apart before our very eyes, you little twit? Are you oblivious to everything?*

With a shake of her head, Amara approached the wash basin, hoping the tepid water would invigorate her. After scrubbing her face she let her hair down and then picked up the porcelain hairbrush and started tugging through the thick tresses. She pondered her reflection in the mirror as she counted the strokes. Her cheekbones appeared more prominent than usual. Smudges under her lower lashes, attesting to her lack of sleep, intensified the deep blue of her eyes. She was thinner all around except for her bosom, amazingly enough. *When did that happen?* she thought as she scrutinized herself more thoroughly.

"Lookin' to see if ye've aged overnight?" came a voice softly from the doorway.

Amara spun around, her cheeks pinkening.

"I know I certainly have aged, but ye don't look a day over eighteen," her father said, his voice barely above a whisper. He opened up his arms to her. "Happy birthday, lass."

"Thank you, Father," she replied, throwing herself into his arms. No matter how chaotic the world outside was, Amara always felt secure in her father's embrace. "Is it really the second of September today?"

"That it is."

Taking her hand, her father led her to the kitchen. "I've got a present fer ye. It's been tucked safely away fer months waitin' fer this special day."

A bolt of cloth laid across the table shimmered in the early morning light. Stepping closer, Amara reached out to caress the fabric, blinking back her tears. The material was gossamer thin and a brilliant shade of blue.

"I couldn't help but think of yer pretty eyes when I saw this. The Widow Thompson came te me several months ago looking te barter this fer more practical goods. Hopefully ye'll find the time te fashion this into a garment fer yer trousseau."

*My trousseau?* Not that long ago Amara had fantasized of meeting the man of her dreams, being offered his hand in marriage, and living happily ever after. The longer the war dragged on, the less likely that prospect seemed. *Why bother working on my trousseau when I'll probably end up being an old maid anyway,* thought Amara morosely.

Setting that consideration aside, she put a smile on her face, swept the fabric into her arms and turned to her father.

"Thank you so much, Father. It's the most gorgeous cloth I've ever seen. It will make a fetching gown. I'll think of you every time I wear it."

"I look forward te seein' ye in it, darlin'."

Placing a kiss on his worn cheek, Amara left the room to find a spot to conceal her gift where Theresa wouldn't stumble across it. She pried open her hope chest and lovingly placed it between the folds of a quilt.

The thought of that beautiful hidden treasure picked up her spirits as Amara walked through the quiet city streets to the hospital. The folks who hadn't abandoned the city seemed to be waiting in anticipation. For what, Amara didn't know and chances were they didn't either.

At the infirmary, people went about their business like any other day—rounds were conducted by Uncle William, orderlies rearranged cots, a meal was being prepared—yet a sense of unease permeated the building. Amara felt jittery as she tended to her patients. After dropping the third item that morning, she determined a break was in order so she could calm her nerves. The shady front porch seemed just the place for a retreat. A wicker chair looked inviting and she sank into it, taking her first deep breath of the day.

From a distance Amara could hear the strains of music. As it got closer she could distinguish the melody of "*The Battle Hymn of the Republic.*" Fear struck her heart. *Are the Yankees in our city?* Rising from her chair, she positioned herself next to one of the porch columns, straining her eyes to see beyond the eastern edge of the square. Neighboring residents filtered out of their houses, keeping wary eyes on the street as well.

As the music increased in volume, soldiers turned onto the square, marching in precision, six abreast. When the first row of men turned onto the street in front of the hospital, the cavalry units bringing up the rear became visible.

Try as she might, Amara could not look away from the scene unfolding before her eyes. Like the other townsfolk, she watched in silence as the soldiers paraded by. When the mounted soldiers drew up, ramrod straight in their saddles, plumes proudly crowning their hats, Amara willed herself to walk back into the hospital, but her feet would not obey her.

She couldn't help but look at the profiles of the men, hoping to God none of Michael's former classmates were part of this debacle. The soldiers proceeded in order from lowest rank to highest.

As the sergeants approached, Amara squinted into the sun and put up her hand to shade her eyes. A soldier on the end of a row facing her side of the street caught her eye. With his height and faultless posture, he stood out from the other men. He looked like he was born in the saddle, gently guiding the raven-colored horse down the thoroughfare. Something about him looked familiar. *That man has an uncanny resemblance to Nathan.*

As the horse and rider were about to pass, the man turned slightly towards Amara. She blinked her eyes and looked at the man again. Her ears began to ring as she leaned against the column for support.

*It was him.* While he was now clean-shaven, his face was one Amara would never forget. She stared at his back until he was no longer in sight. *What was Corporal Nathan Simmons of the Confederate Army doing riding in a Union cavalry unit through the middle of Atlanta, bedecked in the blue uniform of a Federal sergeant?*

Then it hit her. *Jesus, Mary, Joseph. Nathan is a spy for the Union Army.*

The ringing in Amara's ears became a roar, bright and dark spots flickered before her eyes, and then suddenly everything went black.

***

The reception of the Union soldiers by the citizens of Atlanta was generally what Nathan had anticipated. The people who had lined the streets looked on with expressions ranging from fear to distrust to resignation, yet no one dared express their feelings out loud.

Nathan had jockeyed his horse to the far side of the ranks before entering the city so he could gain the best vantage of the hospital. He was hoping Amara would be outside the building and he could get one last glimpse of her to engrave in his memory. There was no chance of them ever being together again—Southern women did not fraternize with Union soldiers, period. It was grounds for disownment by their families and ostracism by the community.

As they had executed the ninety-degree turn onto Capital Square, Nathan's heart skipped a beat when he spied Amara and several other workers on the front porch of the hospital. Even with her eyes shaded, the trim figure and mane of auburn hair distinguished her from the other women. She appeared to be searching for someone as she systematically inspected each row of soldiers.

Nathan focused his eyes straight ahead. As his horse trotted past the front gate of the hospital, he could sense a pair of eyes locked on him. Instinctively he knew it was Amara. He couldn't stop himself and took a slight look to his right.

A brief glance was all it took for Nathan to discern that he had been recognized. Amara's eyes had widened and her hand flew up to cover her mouth. The look on her face was one of horror.

Immediately Nathan was filled with remorse for his foolish action. Lord knew what Amara must be thinking.

***

From the doorway, Doc saw Amara slumped on the ground and came to her assistance.

"Bring me a cool compress," barked Doc to a nurse walking through the foyer.

"Amara, wake up." The doctor cradled her head in the crook of his left arm and gently tapped her cheek with two fingers. Her eyes slowly fluttered open as she tried to focus on her uncle's worried visage. A nurse handed the doctor a wet rag, which he applied to his niece's forehead.

"I know it's a shock to witness Union soldiers marching through our streets, but you mustn't let them see you like this. We need to show them what Southern women are made of."

"Of course, Uncle," said Amara as she struggled to right herself. "I'm sorry I reacted so poorly. It's just..."

"No need to apologize, dear. Let's get you on your feet and when the ensemble is completely past, we'll have someone take you home. You've been working yourself to exhaustion these past few days. A decent rest will do you a world of good."

Nodding her head, Amara let her uncle hand her off to Jeb Sampson, the man who did odd jobs around the hospital. She was deposited onto the cushioned back seat of the carriage. Jeb hobbled over to the other side of the vehicle, pulled himself up to the driver's seat, grabbed the reins and set the horse off in the direction of McKirnan Dry Goods.

Amara stared out the window as they clipped along while the scene she just witnessed played over and over again in her mind. The more she thought about it, the more incensed she became. *I can't believe I let that man play me for a fool,* she fumed. *How could I let his handsome looks blind me to his hideous character?*

After seething over the whole situation for several more blocks, Amara slowly came to a decision. She wasn't going to devote any more time to the rat. "That blackguard means nothing to me," she exclaimed to herself, stamping her heel down to emphasize the point. *No matter what it takes, I'm going to erase the memory of that abysmal creature from my head.*

It was apparent from the trampled road that they were following the tracks of the Union troops. As they approached the store, Amara turned her thoughts to more pressing matters. She wondered about her father's reaction to the invading forces. *I can't imagine how Father kept his anger in check as the soldiers went by. He must be furious.*

When they arrived, Amara thanked Jeb for the ride and assured him she would be perfectly fine and there was no need for him to walk her into the house. With his stringy hair, pock-marked face and hunched carriage, he reminded her of a giant rodent himself. He had a way of looking at her with his dark squinty eyes that made her uncomfortable. She was feeling out of sorts as it was and had no desire to spend any more time with him than necessary.

As he departed, Amara noticed the door to the store was ajar. She approached it, wondering what state her father would be in.

Stepping across the threshold, Amara let her eyes adjust to the muted interior.

"Father? Are you in here?"

When no one answered, Amara made her way to the back of the building to enter their living quarters. As she passed the counter along the back wall, she tripped on something jutting out from behind the enclosure.

Amara turned to see what snagged her foot and her heart sank. It was her father's arm. He must have fallen.

"Father, are you all right?" She knelt down alongside him. His eyes were open and he had a stricken look on his face. His left hand clutched his chest and his brow was damp with perspiration.

"No. Oh God, no!" Amara put her middle and forefinger to her father's jugular vein and felt only a slight movement.

"Please, Father, no. Don't leave me." Amara gently shook her father's shoulders, trying to get a response from him. "I cannot bear to lose one more person."

"Amara, darlin'," came the hoarse reply.

"Yes, Father."

"Ye need te stay strong, there be people dependin' on ye."

"I don't think I can."

"Ye can and ye must. Ye're of sturdy Irish stock. Ye can do anything ye put yer mind te." His voice grew faint. "I'll be seein' yer mother today. I'll tell her what a fine young woman ye've become."

Amara's vision was blurred by tears. She tried to swallow the lump in her throat. "Tell her I love her and I miss her terribly. I love you too, Father."

"Ye've been me beloved since the moment I laid eyes on ye, Amara, and ye always will be."

The sobs came over Amara in waves as the beating of his heart faded away beneath her fingertips.

# Chapter XVII

The hot weather called for hasty funeral arrangements. The lack of household help meant that Amara had to fetch Father O'Reilly herself. After the anointing of the body, she asked the priest to help carry her father's remains to the cellar to keep cool. It was humiliating, but Amara didn't think her stepmother had the ability to lift that much weight, and Theresa had already expressed a distaste for being in the vicinity of a corpse.

Both Theresa and Mrs. McKirnan had been less than helpful since the news of the man's death. They viewed the body, said their goodbyes and, much to Amara's dismay, immediately went in search of needle, thread and father's most expensive black silk fabric to prepare their mourning gowns. As per usual, James was nowhere to be found.

Amara notified her uncle and their few remaining neighbors, figuring word would spread quickly enough to her father's other acquaintances who were still in the city. Digging through the chest in her bedroom, she found the mourning dress that had been in storage since the year of her mother's passing. Trying it on, Amara discovered it was four inches above her ankles and the bodice was too snug for comfort, but it was black, as protocol dictated. She doubted she could stand wearing it for six hours, let alone six months. If time permitted later, she would loosen the side seams and add a strip of fabric to the bottom to lengthen the piece.

Knowing that sleep would be impossible unless she was completely exhausted, Amara kept at her tasks, preparing for the morrow, until she could keep her eyes open no longer. She trudged to bed and slept like the dead herself, with nary a dream disturbing her slumber.

Upon awakening, Amara's disorientation caused her to wonder if she had made up all the events of the previous day. Spying Theresa's new black gown hanging from a peg, reality washed over her. *How could a day start out so wonderfully and end so tragically?*

The priest was kind enough to arrive early for the service so he could help get the body up to the parlor for the showing. Escorting Fr. O'Reilly to the cellar, Amara made a mental note to clip more flowers from the garden to place in the parlor as the rapidly decomposing body smelled rather foul.

Seeing the task before them, she surmised it was going to be a greater struggle to bring the remains up the set of stairs than it had been going down.

It was more than Amara could deal with at that moment. She asked Fr. O'Reilly to wait a minute so she could run to one of the neighboring houses to see if she could find someone to help. She had to knock on three doors before anyone answered. The boy in the doorway was an adolescent, but built soundly enough and willing to be of assistance.

It took the two males several minutes to make their way up the stairs. When Fr. O'Reilly finally backed up the last step his face was beet red, and his receding hairline revealed a forehead dotted with sweat. His gasping breath made Amara fear for his own health by the time the body was laid upon the dining room table.

Amara was grateful to see that Mrs. McKirnan had scrounged up what food she could find to prepare a small repast for their guests. James had finally stumbled in during the wee hours of the morning and managed to make himself look respectable before the first visitors arrived.

Clothed in matching mourning apparel, both mother and daughter seemed more distraught at the wake than they had a day earlier. Perhaps they were over their shock and the reality of losing the patriarch of the family was setting in, Amara speculated.

"This wretched war has taken my beloved husband from me," wailed Mrs. McKirnan, dabbing her eyes with a lacy handkerchief, as she was comforted by an elderly neighbor. "Whatever shall I do?"

"*Mon Papa, mon Papa,*" moaned Theresa, from just inside the parlor entrance, tears welling in her delicate blue eyes.

Not one tear had fallen from Amara's eyes since she bade her father goodbye the previous afternoon. She stood tall and courteously greeted the handful of well-wishers. People remarked on her composure as she serenely performed her duties, but her tranquil facade belied the flurry of thoughts going through her head.

The words from their friends were comforting, but Amara was glad when the last farewells were spoken. Thankfully, the undertaker interrupted his hospital rounds to remove her father's body that afternoon. The burial would take place when a casket became available and when a plot could be unearthed at the church cemetery.

With all those details taken care of, Amara finally had a few minutes to think. As chaotic as wartime was, she had maintained a routine over the last several months. Her days were spent at the hospital and her evenings had been devoted to her duties at home. She cleaned up after the meal, fetched water from the well to wash the dishes, swept the first floor and then put her head to her father's account books.

Now she needed to figure out what to do with her family and the business. "There be people dependin' on ye," her father had told her in his final moments. *People depending on me, but on whom am I to depend?*

"Amara, we need to have a discussion."

She briefly closed her eyes and took a deep breath. She hadn't thought the topic would come up this quickly. "Yes, Mrs. McKirnan," she said, turning to face her stepmother.

"We must talk about selling your father's business and leaving town," said the woman matter-of-factly.

It took a moment for the words to sink in. "Sell the business? To whom? The local citizenry is abandoning town faster than rats deserting a sinking ship. There won't be any negotiating with those Yankees occupying the city. They'll just take anything they want."

Her stepmother's silence gave Amara the momentum to continue. "And where shall we go? We have no kin waiting for us to show up on their doorstep."

"Perhaps we can't sell the business, but I am not of a mind to wait here until the Yankees come pounding on our door."

The thought of walking away from the business into which her father had poured his life sickened Amara. "Do you have some plan in mind?"

"Well, we could go north to one of the Border States," said Mrs. McKirnan. "We'll take what money we have and find a place to stay until the war is over."

"Our money? Confederate currency? It's not worth the price of the paper on which it's printed," Amara said in disgust. "Have you noticed lately that a loaf of bread costs nearly one hundred dollars? We'd be destitute before a week was out."

"If you're so smart, young lady, what do you propose we do?"

Amara considered the question for a few seconds. "I think we need to stay put. At least we have a roof over our heads and a garden yielding produce. Hopefully the Yanks won't see value in requisitioning our property. With any luck, this occupation will be temporary."

Brave words but Amara wasn't sure she believed them

herself. Working at the hospital, she was privy to more military information that most Atlantians. Things weren't going well for the South. The capture of Atlanta could be the final blow for the young nation. While some of the Union soldiers were said to be ruthless, the riffraff outside the municipality were even more feared as they answered to no one. They preyed on the innocent refugees attempting to take flight from the city.

"Fine, we'll stay then," snapped her stepmother. "But Theresa and I will have our valises packed and at the ready should circumstances call for a hasty exit."

"That sounds like the prudent thing to do, Mrs. McKirnan."

With the issue resolved for the time being, Amara made her way to the storefront. She needed to empty the shelves. No use tempting fate by leaving any wares visible for the occupying soldiers to see.

Once all the goods were safely stored in the small attic above her bedroom, one item still remained to be dealt with. Amara looked at the derringer in her palm. Her father had it tucked away behind the store counter to discourage miscreants from making off with any of his merchandise. Amara clicked open the chamber to see if the shot was still in place. As she expected, the firearm had never been discharged.

Guns made her uneasy but, as their family owned a business, one was a necessary evil. Amara decided to slip it into the bottom of her hope chest. No need to tell the others of its whereabouts. James would never be able to reach it quickly enough to defend the household, and Amara didn't trust either her stepmother or stepsister handling the object. They were more likely to shoot each other than a marauding soldier.

With those tasks behind her, Amara went to bed to catch a few hours of sleep.

# Chapter XVIII

The next morning Amara arose with the sun so she could get to the hospital before the city began to stir. She took the back way to avoid running into patrols.

One positive result of the Confederate evacuation was a lull in fighting in the Atlanta area. When Amara arrived at the hospital, only a few staff members roamed the property. It dawned on her that these may be the only workers left. Tales of plunder and rape had scared off the other female personnel. Most of the males had vanished as well, save the few who were too old to travel and, to Amara's dismay, Jeb Sampson.

Locating her uncle on the second floor of the building, she asked him for a moment of his time.

"Absolutely, dear. With so few cots filled, we'll find adequate privacy in the corner of the room," he said, leading her across the floor. "I'm very happy to see you today but surprised you are back so soon."

"I need to tell you something," Amara said hesitantly. A look of concern came to her uncle's face.

"Not more bad news, I hope."

"Not that kind of bad news," said Amara emphatically, thinking back to the lists of men's names posted in the town square.

She took a deep breath in. "I hate to have to tell you this, sir, but I'm afraid I must curtail my work here."

To Amara's surprise, the man nodded his head in a knowing fashion. "I had a feeling this day would arrive before long. How did you come to this decision?"

"I cannot keep fooling myself," said Amara. "The streets of Atlanta aren't safe anymore. I feel terrible putting James at risk accompanying me here and back. Besides, with the Federal troops occupying the city, the skirmishes around the area are nearly nonexistent and we have fewer patients. When Sherman and his army depart, the capital will once again be in the hands of its municipal government. At that point, I plan on returning as I should be able to traverse the streets without concern."

"It's obvious you've thought this through, Amara. Can I talk you into staying for the day and tying up some loose ends before your sabbatical?"

"I would be more than happy to do that, sir."

Amara took her leave from the man and exited the ward. As she walked down the stairs, she compiled a list in her head of the items that most needed her attention before she left.

Over the next few hours, Amara restocked supplies, sterilized and organized equipment, filed papers and completed medical ledgers.

As the afternoon drew to a close, she glanced out the office window and noticed a number of Federal officers tying their mounts to the hitching post in front of the hospital.

Apprehensively, Amara made her way to the front entryway, straightening her skirt as she went. She opened the door just as a soldier was raising his hand to pull the door chime.

"Pardon me, Miss," said the corporal, sweeping his hat from his head. "We are here to talk to Doctor William Burgess."

"Please step in, sir. I will tell him he has visitors."

Amara dashed to the back of the house in search of her uncle. *What could the Union Army possibly want with him?*

When she located the doctor, she accompanied him to the front portal, standing nearby as he politely greeted the six men now filling the entryway. She could hear the beating of her own heart as she anxiously surveyed the group.

The last man to step forward had an air of authority about him. The stars on his shoulders indicated he was a high-ranking officer. Amara guessed he was in his mid-forties. The beard on his chin was as fiery red as the hair on top of his head.

"Major General William Tecumseh Sherman," said the man, stretching out his hand.

Doc shook the man's hand, a baffled look on his face.

"*The* Major General William Tecumseh Sherman?"

"The one and only as far as I know," said the man dryly. "Dr. Burgess, my men and I are conducting a tour of the hospitals in the city. I've heard excellent reports of your facility."

"Thank you, sir," said Doc, still trying to comprehend the situation. "However, I must give credit where credit is due. I have an excellent staff, including my niece Amara," he mentioned, indicating the girl behind him, "who has proven to be invaluable in the administration of this hospital. The men consider her an angel both in the surgical unit and on the floor."

Amara's face blanched as all eyes turned her way.

"Miss..." queried the general.

"Mc-McKirnan, sir," she stammered.

"Very nice to make your acquaintance, Miss McKirnan," he said while executing a slight bow.

"And yours as well," Amara replied automatically. The situation was beyond belief. *Why am I in my uncle's foyer chatting with a group of our mortal enemies?*

"Would you care to see the premises?" Doc inquired of the general.

"I would be much obliged, sir. Miss McKirnan, if you would be so kind as to come with us, we would enjoy your company as well."

"Certainly, sir," said Amara, her ingrained manners automatically surfacing. She walked alongside her uncle as the tour began. Doc encouraged her to point out the various attributes of the hospital that were under her jurisdiction. After a few minutes, she forgot the audience she addressed, and her natural enthusiasm for her vocation surfaced as she pointed out the various amenities of the hospital.

"I've seen exactly what I need to," commented the officer as the excursion concluded.

Doc and Amara looked at the general, unsure of his insinuation.

"This will be the primary Union Army hospital for Fulton County. The care of all injured officers will be conducted on these grounds," said Sherman, before he turned to make his exit. Amara looked at her uncle to gauge his reaction. He appeared as befuddled as she was.

The doors were pulled open and the general paused to conduct one last piece of business.

"Dr. Burgess, you are hereby commissioned a surgeon in the United States Army. You are to remain on these grounds to run this facility until further notice." Doc was generally unflappable but a look of astonishment crossed his face.

"As for you, Miss," continued the solider as he turned his attention to Amara, "seeing how integral your services are to the administration of this hospital, you shall be assigned to this facility as well until further notice."

Amara couldn't help but glance over her shoulder to see if there was some other woman behind her he may have been addressing. Seeing no one, her head snapped back in Sherman's direction. Her mouth opened, but no words came to her tongue.

The good doctor stepped forward to voice the words that evaded Amara.

"Are you telling us, General, that we are under house arrest?" asked the doctor pointedly.

"That could be one way to look at it, Dr. Burgess," said Sherman as he tugged a riding glove onto each hand. "Let us just say that for the time being, you are guests of the Union Army."

He turned sharply and made his way onto the porch, his men behind him in close formation. The last man out soundly shut the door behind the group, leaving the doctor and Amara gaping in utter disbelief.

# Chapter XIX

"How dare he?" seethed Amara when her tongue finally came back to life. "Who does he think he is that he can order a civilian to do his bidding? I'm not one of his minions. I'll be damned if I will obey his commands."

"Amara, before you do anything rash, let's think this through," said Doc prudently, putting his hands on her shoulders. "That man is one of the highest-ranking officers in the Union Army. I doubt if he rose to that position by issuing orders that weren't carried out. He brooks no disobedience."

"If he wants me working in his hospital so badly, he can drag me back here," growled Amara as she shook herself free from her uncle's grasp. She yanked open the door and took one step out only to see a pair of Sherman's soldiers standing at attention, pistols at the ready by their sides.

Amara opened her mouth, then thought better of it and snapped it shut. She stepped back into the building and slammed the offending slab of wood behind her.

"If that man were here right now, I would wrench every last red hair off his head," Amara muttered. "The audacity—forcing a Southern lady to toe the line for some boot-licking, power-hungry Yank bent on pillaging the Confederacy."

Thankfully, the man in question wasn't in the vicinity. If looks could kill, the Union Army would soon be in need of a new commanding officer for the Western Theatre.

Considering his niece closely, Doc guided her towards his office. He sat her down on the settee and then went across the room to his desk. He pulled out writing materials and proceeded to compose a note. When the paper was signed, he showed it to Amara for her perusal and then left the room, calling out for Jeb as he departed.

Amara could hear the man directing Jeb to deliver the missive to Mrs. McKirnan so she would be aware of her stepdaughter's whereabouts.

As the two concluded their business in the hallway, the sound of books slamming to the floor reverberated throughout the first floor.

"Sounds like Amara is giving the office a good cleaning," said Doc wryly.

Clouds of dust puffed up as each manual hit its mark. Amara pictured every book with a face and a sprout of red hair as she yanked it off the shelf and pitched it at the planks of wood beneath her feet. When the shelves were all cleared and she calmed down some, she began the task of righting the room and cleaning it properly.

The hospital benefited from her newfound vigor. No spot was missed as Amara attacked every speck of dirt she could find over the next twenty-four hours, grumbling under her breath as she worked. A cot was set up in the office and when all her energy was spent, she collapsed upon it for a few hours of sleep before resuming her vigorous assault on unsuspecting grime.

Even the attic reaped the rewards of her vengeance. From the looks of it, no one had stepped foot in the place since she and her brothers last played there as children. The dust was so thick that Amara had to cover her nose with the hem of her apron to keep from sneezing as she swept the floor.

Being in that space brought a host of memories to mind for Amara. She paused as they washed over her. Countless games of hide-and-seek were played in this very house. *Michael was always the logical one*, she thought with a slight smile. He hid in spots he assumed she wouldn't be willing to check, like the dark and dank cellar. Regardless of her distaste for creepy-crawly things, Amara wouldn't let a few nasty little creatures stand in her way of winning a game.

James was truly the clever one. Amara could recall futilely searching for him on many an occasion. When she eventually gave in and asked for a hint, his voice always seemed to come from the attic. She'd race up the stairs and search the space from top to bottom to no avail. Inevitably she would next hear him calling her name from below the attic window and would see him in the backyard laughing like a jackal. How infuriated she would be. *It still irks me that I never figured out how he managed to do that.* Now that she thought of it again, she'd have to bring the subject up with James when she next saw him.

With a sigh, Amara went back to work. Once the floor was adequately swept, she took the broom and ran it across the ceiling and up and down each wall to snag the cobwebs clinging to the surfaces. She hoped the occupants of the webs were long gone.

Clearing the far wall of the room, the broom stopped in mid sweep as some of the bristles caught on the wood. Amara gave the broom a solid tug, heard a click and nearly took a tumble backwards when the broom disengaged from the wall. Steadying herself, she noticed a space between two wall studs. Pushing on the panel, Amara saw it was actually a narrow door. When it creaked fully opened, she could see the top of a set of circular stairs.

The realization dawned on her. *The sneak! That's how he did it. All this while I thought he was a master of the game hide-and-seek.* She had no doubt the steps led out to the grounds surrounding the house. *Wait until I see James again and tell him I've discovered his ruse.*

She was curious to traverse the stairway to see exactly how they fit into the floor plan, but with no lantern in hand, Amara would have to save her exploration for another day. *I will have plenty of time to figure out all the secrets of this house since I shan't be permitted to leave in the foreseeable future.*

A revelation came to her as she pondered that thought. *'Tis better to beg forgiveness than ask permission, is it not? Maybe I will be able to take a leave of absence from my post here.*

Amara secured the passageway and gathered her cleaning supplies. The first shipment of Union officers was set to arrive in the morning. She wasn't sure what condition the men would be in, as all were being shipped from other hospitals in the county. But beds had to be made and supplies organized for what would no doubt be a taxing day.

As much as Amara needed to sleep that night, she tossed and turned as thoughts of family members ran through her head. James may have been bright as a child but, at this point in his life, was he wise enough to keep to the house? Was Mrs. McKirnan still mourning or was she already spinning the web for her next prey? Has Theresa finally opened her eyes and realized that the life she once knew is over for good, not temporarily set aside? Have the soldiers ignored the unassuming dwelling and left her kinsfolk alone?

When the carriages and buckboards began to roll up just as the sun was breaking the horizon, she felt as if she hadn't had a wink of sleep. Abandoning the idea of any more rest, she quickly dressed and went out to meet the drivers. The first priority was getting the patients with life-threatening conditions into surgery. Some procedures, such as the removal of a precariously embedded shot, were too delicate to be performed in the field hospitals. Amara, with her long, slender fingers, made the ideal surgical assistant. If Doc determined that the point of entry was too small for a forceps to be inserted, he would have Amara use her pincer grasp to secure the offending article. Working her way through flesh and blood vessels was far from her favorite task, but she knew it needed to be done and she seemed to have an aptitude for it.

The conveyances trickled in throughout the day. After ten hours in the surgical ward, Amara was finally able to retreat to the office, have a bite to eat and rest her weary back for a few minutes. The most severe cases had been dealt with and she intended to check on the other men later. *Confederate or Union, all men look the same on the operating table*, she mused. She was heartened that they were able to save most of those poor souls whose lives were in their hands this day.

Walking through the wards that evening, Amara saw many patients there for the purpose of recuperation rather than surgery. Loss of sight and loss of limbs afflicted a good portion of the men she inspected. Until this point the hospital staff's focus had been on patching up men as best they could and shipping them out posthaste. Helping the unfortunates learn to live with their disfigurements was something in which she had scant experience, other than assisting James.

Amara searched her uncle out to discuss the matter with him. He was in his office, leaning back in his chair with his feet up on his desk, leisurely smoking a cigar. Amara couldn't resist his offer of a cup of strong coffee. She basked in its entrancing aroma, savoring each sip. After more time than she could recall of drinking hickory coffee, this was certainly a treat. She felt a smidgen guilty as this coffee was procured from the stores intended for the Union soldiers. But, after all, she was a *guest* of the United States Army. She was certain they would be happy to share their bounty with her.

"We need to secure equipment for the men to get them

back on their feet," said Doc. "The only person with a stock of lumber at this point is the undertaker. I will send Jeb over there tomorrow to scrounge up whatever's available so we can fashion crutches in the workshop here.

"What of the men who have lost both legs?" asked Amara.

"We've plenty of straight-backed chairs. We can bring them to the wagon shop and have the proprietor convert them to wheeled-chairs. The men need to accustom themselves to these ambulatory supports to get around and now is just as good of a time as later."

Doc leaned over to dip his fountain pen in the ink well and scratched a few notes on a piece of paper. Looking up at Amara, he continued. "Your help will be needed for the men who have lost a hand or arm, particularly if it is their dominant appendage. Do what you can to be of assistance, but gradually turn the process over to them so they can learn to care for themselves."

Amara nodded in assent. "What of the blind men, sir?"

"That is a difficult proposition. They too need to learn to fend for themselves. The best you can do is aid them in conquering the tasks they'll face on a daily basis. Things as simple as shaving, feeding themselves or finding their way to the privy will be of utmost importance. That's really all we can do for them."

It seemed like a daunting job to Amara, but if it could help someone regain a semblance of their former life, she was willing to put in the effort it would take to work with these patients. "Thank you for putting your confidence in me, sir."

"It's well-placed, I'm sure. Now off to sleep with you, it's going to be a long day tomorrow."

"Goodnight, Doc."

"Goodnight, dear."

# Chapter XX

As the doctor had predicted, the next day was a tedious one for Amara. It was the start of countless days of difficult, heart-wrenching work. There were so many men looking for assistance and so few minutes to spend with each one. Every time one soldier was readied for departure, another man stood in queue, awaiting his space.

The Union officers were, for the most part, an educated lot and thus heading back to civilian jobs devoid of manual labor. Career soldiers would be assigned to office duties through the military. The most difficult cases for Amara were the men who lived off the land and needed to be able to support their families. *What kind of living could they make if they are no longer able-bodied?* She did what she could for them during the several days they were allotted to work together, and said a prayer for each man as they walked, or were wheeled, out of her presence for the last time.

One particular gentleman touched her heart because he reminded her so of her father. Major Charles Wescott, of the Wescotts of Great Falls, New Hampshire had lost his left leg in the battle at Allatoona. On the third day of his stay, Amara was assigned to help him maneuver about on his freshly-issued crutches. He wasn't having any of it.

"I've told you of the striking resemblance you bear to my father, haven't I?" Amara asked as she tried to persuade him to bear his weight on the crutches.

"I recall hearing something of it," he replied cantankerously.

"Well, you're as stubborn as the day is long, just as he was."

"Hmpf. I would hope he didn't stand for any of that kind of talk from you, young lady."

"I'm just telling you the truth, sir. Now let's be cooperative and stand up nice and straight and try to take a step or two, shall we? You need to prove to Doc that you're mobile so we can send you home."

"Send me home to what? I've spent my entire military career on a saddle. I saw my first taste of war in '32 during the Blackhawk War in Illinois. We went from there straight down to Florida to fight the Second Seminole War and I haven't looked back since. What kind of life will I have? The thought of sitting behind a desk all day shuffling papers makes me want to pierce my heart with my own dagger," he said bitterly. "If I could find the damnable thing," he added in an annoyed tone as he pulled up the sheet to check the foot of the bed.

"What kind of talk is that?" admonished Amara. She smoothed the bedding back into place. "Don't you have a family waiting for your return?"

"Family? Who has time for a family when you spend your life gallivanting hither and yon at the whims of Uncle Sam?"

"Maybe now is the time to think of settling down," said Amara gently. "There's bound to be some widows in Great Falls looking for some company. A man with your fine looks will be sure to catch some lady's eye."

The man considered Amara's statement for a bit. "Give me those crutches. I'll be damned if I am going to crawl back to my birthplace."

After thirty minutes of slowly walking forward, executing turns, and balancing in front of a washstand with Amara hovering nearby, the man looked tired but was pleased with himself. Without thinking, Amara threw her arms around the major's waist, careful not to bowl him over with her enthusiasm.

"I'm so proud of you. I can just see you now, strolling

into Great Falls with your head held high. That will be one magnificent day."

"Indeed it will," he replied, drawing back from Amara a bit. His eyebrows narrowed and he tilted his head down to look her directly in the eye.

"Young lady, if you are going to get that familiar with all the men here there will be a line forming down the length of the hall for your ministrations. I would suggest you keep a professional attitude at all times, especially around these rascals."

"Of course, sir," replied Amara, doing her best to refrain from saluting.

Even though she knew he was joshing her, Amara kept that thought in mind as she worked with the men. She did her best not to get close with any of them. It wasn't as easy as it would seem. In her mind, she knew these soldiers were trespassers in her city, but Amara couldn't deny the compassion she held for them in her heart. Most felt they were fighting to keep the country united and were convinced God was on their side. The thought of battling their own countrymen was a troubling one and they looked forward to peace reigning over the country once again.

Amara didn't remember exactly when it happened or if it was even one particular incident, but it occurred to her one day that she had become color blind. She no longer saw the blue trousers and jackets the soldiers wore. All she saw were men in need of repair, and repair them was exactly what she was going to do to the best of her abilities.

# Chapter XXI

Nathan looked for an opportunity to make his way back to the hospital to plead his case with Amara but, as the days went by, he never had the chance. His unit was given the job of securing any goods from the warehouse district that had escaped the flames of the retreating Confederate troops. When not scavenging, the men patrolled the streets, per orders of their colonel.

On the seventh day of September, Sherman called for the civilian evacuation of Atlanta. Nathan was in one of the details assigned to post notices around the city. Citizens gathered around the bills, vehemently protesting the order. General Hood rode into town ahead of a contingent of soldiers to confront Sherman. Seeing the furious look on Hood's face, Nathan instructed the men around him to follow the group to their destination and keep an eye on the proceedings.

Hood pounded on the door of Sherman's headquarters. Having been forewarned, Sherman swung open the door himself.

"What reason have you to force Atlanta's citizens to evacuate?" bellowed Hood, looking his adversary directly in the eye. "You have control of the city, what more do you need?"

"A little privacy to start," said Sherman, glancing at the gathering crowd. "Won't you please step in?"

"Dispense with the bull, Sherman. "What are your intentions?"

"I mean to see an end to this war," said Sherman, the conviction evident in his tone. "Jeff Davis can't get past his pride and look at the reality of this situation. There will be no victory for the South. I intend to burn a swath from Atlanta to the Gulf of Mexico. When the Confederacy is cut in two there will be no choice but to surrender."

"Are you mad?" Hood said, with his anger barely held in check. "I never thought I'd live to see the day when a fellow West Point graduate would stoop so low. Have you no compassion for innocent human beings?"

"I've given them fair warning, have I not?"

"You call twenty-four hours fair warning?" Hood sputtered.

"Shall we say a week, then?"

Hood stood his ground as he appeared to be mentally sorting through the available options.

Sherman was well-known for his stubborn nature. The chances of anyone convincing him to change his course of action in general were notoriously slim but, in matters of war, were virtually non-existent.

"Ten days, no less," spat out Hood.

With that he spun on his heel, stormed down the steps and mounted his horse. Reining the animal around to face Sherman, he left with one parting shot.

"You like fire so much? I hope to God you burn in hell, you bastard."

"My best to you too, Hood." Sherman said as he retreated into the building, pushing the door shut soundly behind him.

Nathan watched as Hood and his men galloped away and considered the significance of the conversation he just witnessed. A person could hardly blame the general for being infuriated; the thought of the senseless loss of property, crops and potentially lives didn't sit well with Nathan either. *Yet, Sherman could be right, this may just be the final push to bring this war to a conclusion,* he reflected.

When the burning would begin, it was hard to say.

Sherman played his cards close to the chest. But the troops were instructed to initiate the evacuation process to get every citizen out of the city within the agreed-upon time frame. *Amara will surely be among the people leaving,* Nathan assumed. His chest tightened at the thought of seeing her one last time.

He was in the contingent of soldiers assigned to overlook the northern evacuation route from the city. Women, children, the aged and the infirm shuffled by, barely looking at the soldiers lining the road. Nathan didn't expect these downtrodden people to create any disturbances so it was a relatively easy assignment. He occupied his time searching the faces of the crowds in hopes of spotting Amara. As the days passed, there was no sign of her which led Nathan to wonder if she and her family had departed using one of the other routes.

When the city was secured, the troops were sent back in the field. Nathan's former regiment, The Army of Tennessee, was determined to disrupt Sherman's supply lines. They were a wily bunch, stealthily destroying sections of train tracks from one end of northern Georgia to the other. Nathan was part of a select band of men commissioned to track down the vigilantes.

From the end of September through October, their group crisscrossed the state. When one fire was extinguished, another flared up. The mounted Federal Army units were sent from Acworth to Flat Creek, Lovejoy Station, Rome and Tunnel Hill. After the ruffians cleared out, all that was left in their wake were mangled rail lines and frustrated Union soldiers. The Confederates consistently managed to stay one pace ahead of their counterparts. Familiarity with the land gave them the upper hand.

Nathan tried to step into the mind of his former officers and figure out what their next move would be. For the life of him he could not decipher their pattern, if there even was one. *How are they choosing their targets?* Abernathy was the analytical type. War to him was a chess match. *What's your next move, Colonel?*

By the first week of November, both men and beasts were exhausted. They had been on a wild goose chase after Hood's rabble-rousers and no end was in sight. When their scout spotted billows of smoke rising beyond the horizon one afternoon, they knew the Rebs were up to no good again.

"It looks like they are up in Adairsville," noted the scout.

"We cannot keep chasing these vagrants," said Nathan as the men gathered together. "We need to determine their next destination." He mentally ticked off the targets that had been hit since they started this game, trying to figure out the pattern.

All at once, it was before his very eyes.

"Saddle up, they're heading to Allatoona."

The men looked at Nathan skeptically.

"And exactly how'd you come about this knowledge, Simmons?" asked First Sergeant Thaddeus Johnson, putting a plug of tobacco in his cheek.

"Pure logic, sir. I was following their trail in my head and when you list the towns off back to back, it occurred to me that the names were in alphabetical order. I doubt if it's coincidental. That being the case, the next spot would most likely be Allatoona."

"It can't be more than five miles west as the crow flies," noted a corporal, looking in that direction. "But a forest stands between here and there. If we ride due north, we can circumvent the woods, but it will more than double the miles we need to travel."

"But how fast can we travel through that thicket?" asked another man, surveying the property.

"Time is of the essence, men," added a third man, looking towards the setting sun. "The Rebs will expect us to sweep in from the north while they hightail it south. If we take the shortest route we may intercept them. The horses can make their way through the underbrush; they've grown accustomed to it."

"We'll take to the woods," commanded Johnson, turning his horse due west.

Nathan nudged his mount after the others but felt a sense of unease as they entered the forest single file. The mare seemed skittish picking her way over roots and fallen branches. They drove on as quickly as they could. The sun was heading close to the horizon when their destination came into sight.

Suddenly, seemingly out of nowhere, a single shot sounded and the lead rider slumped over his horse's neck.

"Rebs!" shouted a panicked voice. "Take cover!"

Pandemonium struck as more shots were fired and the horses reared up in fear, some unseating their riders and bolting out of the trees.

Nathan grabbed his pistol, straining to see their assailants. Bullets rained in around him. He quickly slid off Kalona's back to make himself less vulnerable. She galloped away.

*Where are those devils?* Nathan flattened himself next to a tree trying to determine from which direction the shots were coming. He noticed the other men doing the same. A creaking branch made him look up. *Holy Mother of God, they're in the trees.*

Praying he'd find a straight path through the branches, Nathan trained his weapon at the man stationed a dozen feet above his head. His aim was true and he dodged the body as it fell to the ground.

"They're above you, men. Look up!" All eyes looked skyward and guns were pointed accordingly. The tempo of the shots increased.

Nathan shifted around the tree trunk, hoping to make himself a more elusive target, all the while searching for movement in the treetops. He was able to get off several more successful shots. It was a macabre spectacle, watching men tumble out of their perches to the forest floor.

Pistol held high, another man in his sights, Nathan cocked the gun when a sound exploded nearby and his shooting arm went limp. It felt like he had been hit by a bolt of lightning. He dropped his firearm to the ground and fell to his knees.

*God bless it. Why that arm?* He struggled to pick up the pistol with his left hand. Blood seeped through his jacket as he attempted to steady the piece. Gritting his teeth, trying to keep his focus, he pulled the trigger. Whether he hit his mark or not, he never knew.

What felt like minutes but could have been hours later, Nathan heard someone speaking.

"Sergeant, wake up," a familiar voice was urgently whispering.

*Wake up? That's odd. Why would I be sleeping this time of day?* He tried opening his eyes but his lids were too heavy to budge.

"Sir, we've got to get you out of here." The voice came from far away.

*Get me out of where?* Nathan compelled himself to concentrate. Gradually he became aware of his surroundings. He felt the rough ground beneath him and smelled pine branches. He forced his eyes open to see tree trunks encircling him and a person kneeling by his side.

"Sir, we've got to get you to a doc. You've taken a shot to the upper arm. I stemmed the bleeding for now but you need more help than I can give you."

The details of the skirmish came rushing back to Nathan.

"We were ambushed," he rasped. "How many survived?"

"About a half dozen sir," replied the lieutenant. "But we need to skedaddle out of here. I don't want the Rebs to come back to finish what they started."

The younger man put his arm around Nathan's waist to pull him to his feet. The movement sent shards of pain shooting up his limb. Lightheadedness struck him again and he grabbed onto a tree to steady himself.

"Sir, I've managed to corral one of the horses. We'll have to ride together. There's a field hospital close. I'll get you there as quickly as I can."

Through the fog in his head Nathan recognized Kalona.

"So you didn't abandon me, girl."

The horse stepped forward and nuzzled her master's shoulder.

He allowed himself to be lifted onto the mare and the lieutenant mounted behind him, trying not to unseat his passenger. Nathan endeavored to stay alert but slipped into unconsciousness. He dreamed he was a child again riding with his father, the man's steely arms firmly wrapped around him. The horse came to a halt. *Not yet, Father. One more time around the yard, please?* Two men reached for him. *I don't remember our stable boys being that tall.* Nathan peered at them through his lashes. He was lifted off the horse and carried to a tent.

Once again, he lost consciousness. When he came to, Nathan realized he was lying on a table. The flame from a lantern caused him to squint as his eyes fluttered fully open. A man wearing a blood-soaked apron over an equally soiled shirt poked into his arm, examining his wound. The pain brought Nathan completely awake.

"Looks like the Rebs left you a little souvenir," he said, bending closer to get a better view. He put his index finger into the entry spot, feeling for the shot. Nathan clamped his mouth shut to stop from crying out.

"It's wedged in there, all right. Son, is it hurting you, much?"

"You could say that," he gritted out.

"Well, it's going to hurt a hell of a lot more if gangrene sets in. I'm sorry to say this, but I think it would be best if we took your arm. If the tissue in there starts decaying, you'll be a goner."

The words immediately caused a sense of panic in Nathan. "There's got to be something you can do," he rasped.

"I wish there were, but we don't have the capability here to perform surgeries. Even if we could, there's no guarantee it would be successful." The doctor motioned to a burly orderly to bring him the saw from a nearby stand.

The blood drained from Nathan's face when he spotted the sharp-toothed instrument with rust-colored stains marring its finish. "I have a ranch to run," he panted, terror gripping him. "I need both of my arms to do that. Is there anyone, anywhere who can help me?"

"Son, there's a hospital set up in Atlanta for Sherman's officers. However, between the Confederate scouts and the blood you're apt to lose, you're putting your life at risk even attempting the trip."

"I'd rather die trying than give up. Where's Lieutenant Jacobs? I trust his skill with a gun and a horse," Nathan grated out, his voice losing steam.

"I'm right here, sir," said the man in question, lifting the tent flap. He looked at the saw the orderly wielded. "I'm bringing you to Atlanta, sir. Just hang tight."

A look of relief crossed Nathan's face and he closed his eyes.

"Thank God," he whispered.

The surgeon stood with arms folded, shaking his head. The lieutenant took hold of Nathan's torso and nodded to the orderly to grab his feet.

After Nathan was lifted back onto Kalona, the doctor pulled the officer aside.

"This is foolhardy, you know. You're both going to end up getting killed. Just ride out a ways and back. We'll get him on the gurney and have that arm off before he knows what hit him. It's for his own good."

Through a haze, Nathan heard the words and listened tensely for the response.

"That may be so, sir. But I've given him my word and I intend to stand by it."

After a terse salute, the man swept onto the horse, steadying Nathan in front of him. With a tap of his spurs, he sent the steed flying into the night.

# Chapter XXII

The week had started blessedly slow. A few casualties trickled in, but not nearly the number they saw the previous weeks. Amara looked out the parlor window and counted the wagons pulling up as the sun came into full view. The waves in the glass distorted the view somewhat, giving the scene a dreamlike appearance. *If only this was a dream.*

Three teams of horses were being hitched to the posts in the front yard. A small number, but one never knew what challenges they presented. A sense of foreboding came over her. Fewer vehicles normally meant more severely injured men and more intricate operations.

Amara pulled her shoulders back, took a deep breath, and then headed to the front entry to direct the orderlies with their cargo. The first three men carried in had an ashen pall that foretold imminent death.

"Bring them to the dining room to your right. The man with the head wound, put him on the table. Doc will look at him first. Set the other two on the floor by the window."

The workers nodded and did as they were told, hurrying back to the wagons for the next group.

Amara surveyed the subsequent assembly, noting injuries to the men's appendages. The smell of rotting flesh assaulted her nostrils. *We are not miracle workers here. Why do the field surgeons keep sending us men we can't repair?* Amara bit her lip in frustration. It made no sense prolonging the inevitable. A lost limb was preferable to a lost life.

The orderlies were retrieving their last load when a horse came barreling around the corner of the square, skidding to a halt directly in front of the building. The rider jumped off, pulling his passenger with him, nearly sending both men tumbling to the ground.

Since the orderlies had their hands full, the lieutenant turned to Amara with imploring eyes. "Ma'am, can you please help me get the sergeant inside? He needs to see the doc right away."

"Of course."

Amara ran down the steps and gave the injured man a quick once over. His right shirt sleeve had been torn, revealing a bandaged upper arm. A hat covered his eyes and he was sprouting a stubbly beard. His skin appeared clammy but not deathly gray.

Wrapping her arms around the man's knees, Amara hoisted him up. The rider walked backwards up the steps of the porch, bearing the majority of the weight.

"Go to the back of the house; we'll put him on the table in the kitchen," said Amara, trying to catch her breath. "What's his story?"

"A Reb's bullet is lodged in his arm. The doc says it's right alongside an artery."

"Why wasn't the arm removed?"

"That didn't sit too well with the sergeant, Ma'am. He says he needs both arms to work his property."

"A lot of good that arm will do him when he's six feet under," Amara muttered as she lifted her end of the dead weight onto the table.

After checking his pulse and using the back of her hand to feel his cheek for signs of fever, Amara determined his condition was stable. She instructed his protector to keep an eye on him until she and Doc finished up with the other men in the dining room.

The patient with the head wound had expired in the few minutes she spent tending the sergeant. Doc was doing what he could for the next man up on the table. A blow from a horse's hoof had left the man with internal injuries. Amara slowly administered ether while Doc probed the bruised area to determine the damage.

"He's bleeding somewhere in his gut, I'm most sure of that," said Doc thoughtfully. "We'll have to open him up and see what's amiss."

He ran the edge of a knife over a candle flame to sterilize it. Wiping the blade on his shirt sleeve, he proceeded to make a horizontal incision across the man's midsection, just below the navel. Fortunately he hit pay dirt with the first cut. The stench was overwhelming when a jaggedly severed bowel was revealed.

"Amara, I will piece this back together as well as I can. Your task will be to mop up the debris after I'm done."

"Yes, sir." She assessed the job with a weary and seasoned eye. Not too many months ago listening to the sound of a blade sawing its way through flesh, seeing pus oozing from a man's innards, or being assaulted by the nauseating smell of decomposing intestines would have been too much for her. Now it was just part of her everyday routine.

Twenty-five minutes later, Amara meticulously cleaned the cavity in the man's midsection. When it was adequately taken care of she poured a bit of whiskey in the wound with the hope of fending off contamination. Tidy stitches closed the opening and then she turned the man's care over to the waiting orderly. After a silent Hail Mary was prayed in thanks for the man's survival, she proceeded to the next patient Doc was examining.

They were able to help five of the patients delivered to them that day. Another man died on the table and one man's condition was hopeless. Father O'Reilly was called to administer the Sacrament of the Sick.

With every man accounted for, Doc descended the front steps and made his way to the outdoor pump situated alongside the house. Amara was already there scrubbing her hands with a sliver of lye soap.

"It doesn't get any easier, does it?" asked Amara, inspecting her nails as the water flowed over her fingers.

"What doesn't?" inquired Doc as he bent over to give the well handle a few more pumps.

"Losing them," she said, letting out a sigh.

Doc looked up at her, the compassion showing on his face. "It is war, Amara. It comes with the territory."

"I'm having a hard time of it, Doc. The image of every man I've worked on that we've lost is permanently etched in my mind. They come to me in my dreams, imploring my assistance. The poor man with the head wound this morning, he was gone before..."

In mid-sentence, another man came to mind.

"Oh, Lord."

Picking up her skirts, she turned and ran to the back of the house, bounding up the steps leading to the kitchen two at a time. Thankfully, the man was where she left him, the lieutenant stationed close by. Whether the wounded man was sleeping or passed out, Amara couldn't determine.

"Lieutenant, I'm going to prepare this man for surgery," said Amara, doing her best to compose herself. "Would you be so kind as to go out back and notify Doc that we have another patient on our hands?

"Certainly, Ma'am."

Amara walked over to the cabinet and grabbed a pair of scissors. "We're going to do our best to save your arm, Sergeant, but I'm afraid the shirt is going to be a total loss," she noted, as she started cutting the fabric free from his body. The scissors stopped in mid-snip when she spied a gold crucifix hanging around the man's neck. She couldn't resist picking the cross up and admiring it. While she had done everything she could to erase the memory of

Nathan from her mind, seeing that image of Christ so similar to the one he wore made her think of him. God only knew if he was dead or alive. *Thank you, Lord Jesus, for watching over this soldier. Steady our hands as we work on him. If it be your will, bring him complete healing. Amen.*

Finishing her original task, Amara proceeded to unwrap the bandage covering the man's arm and picked through the dried blood to inspect the wound more closely. It was a clean entry. The skin was singed but not flayed, and, as she had anticipated, there was no exit point. Nothing she hadn't seen countless times before.

"No need for this now, soldier," said Amara, grabbing the edge of his hat with one hand while cradling his head with the other. "Let's set that aside so we can help you go into a nice, deep sleep."

The afternoon light streaming in through the nearby window caused the man to raise his left arm up to cover his eyes.

"We're awake now, are we? Good afternoon," said Amara sweetly.

The soldier lowered his hand and brought his eyes fully open. Amara gasped and dropped his head to the table as if his skull burned her hand.

"Holy Mary, Mother of God. It's *you*," said Amara, taking a step back.

"Amara?" Nathan had a look of confusion on his face.

Gathering her senses, Amara grabbed the scissors from the table and pointed them menacingly in his direction. "It's Miss McKirnan to you, you low-down, yellow-bellied reptile."

Nathan looked at her strangely. "What are you doing here?"

"I work here, you halfwit. The better question is, what are *you* doing here?" hissed Amara. The scissor blades glinted in the sun. "The last time we talked, you were a corporal in the Confederate Army. Imagine my surprise seeing you prancing by this very building with Sherman's troops, riding a Union-issued horse, dolled up in dress blues and sporting sergeant stripes on your sleeve no less."

Building up steam, Amara continued, punctuating each sentence with a shake of the scissors towards Nathan's face. "And to think I nursed you back to health. Me, Amara Elizabeth McKirnan, aiding and abetting a Union solider. Not only a Union soldier, but a Union spy to boot. My father must be spinning in his grave right now."

When she paused for a moment to get a breath, Nathan seized the chance to interject. "Amara, I can explain."

"Like any silver-tongued snake, I'm sure you've concocted a wondrous tale that clarifies how a Confederate corporal miraculously turns into a Union sergeant overnight," said Amara. She yanked a bottle of ether off the shelf. "Save your strength."

The sound of footsteps alerted Amara to the other men's return. She hastily doused ether onto a rag and placed it roughly over Nathan's mouth.

Bending close to his head, she whispered in his ear. "Praise God I'm a Christian woman or this would be the last earthly words you would hear, you traitor."

A scraping noise caused Amara to jerk her head up and look past Nathan. Jeb appeared in the doorway that led from the dining room to the kitchen.

"Will you be wantin' me to fetch the saw?" he asked, scrutinizing the man on the table.

Amara did her best to adopt a composed look as she quickly hid the scissors behind her back. "I don't think that will be necessary. Doc and I will handle this. You may be dismissed."

"Okee Dokee." He turned to leave, words trailing behind him as he walked towards the front of the building.

"Don't know if I'd waste much time on that one."

*How much of our conversation did he hear?* Amara barely had a moment to dwell on that thought as Doc and the lieutenant came in through the back door. She spun around to acknowledge the men.

"He's all ready for surgery, Doc," she said

"Thank you Amara. Let's see what we find here."

Doc grabbed a probe from the countertop and scrutinized the wound. He inserted the instrument at various angles into the opening until he could hear metal connecting with metal.

"It's in there, all right," he noted, squinting to get a better view.

The lieutenant looked to be swaying slightly on his feet.

"May I step outside to get a breath of fresh air?" he asked meekly.

"Certainly, man. We've got everything under control here," said Doc without looking up.

He took one more glance to assess the site.

"I'm going to need you to get this out, Amara," he noted. He looked up at her over his glasses, to ascertain she was listening.

She nodded at him, having surmised his request.

"I'll hold the gap open and you must grab the shot. It's going to be rough going as it's embedded rather deeply."

Amara made the Sign of the Cross and turned her focus to the task in front of her. She gingerly put her index finger into the opening. She felt the shot but the blood surrounding it made it hard to grasp. After several attempts to move the ball, she straightened up. Sweat beaded on her forehead and dripped into her eyes. She dragged her sleeve across her brow, wiped her hands on her apron and dug in again. Finally she was able to dislodge the shot with her fingernail. She urged it closer to the surface until she could get two fingers firmly around it and pull it out.

A sense of relief washed over her. Low-life traitor or not, she couldn't bear to witness one more man die on her watch.

"Wash it out, stitch him up and he should be good as new in no time," said Doc, stretching to get the crick out of his back. "I think our work is done. Excellent job, Amara. When you finish, get yourself some rest. It's been a long day."

"Thank you, sir. I will."

Her respite would come later, however. First she intended to track Jeb down. *I must find out what he heard in my exchange with Nathan—if Nathan's even his real name*, she thought testily. Amara may have lost her faith in the Texan but she had never trusted Jeb. He always seemed to be slithering around the premises. There was something about him that bothered her. She usually tried to avoid him, but she needed to confront him about the disturbing comment he made earlier.

When Amara completed her work on Nathan, she had the orderlies transport him to a cot on the second floor. She then set about locating Jeb. Finding him nowhere in the hospital, she searched the premises. Amara discovered him sitting on the ground next to the stable, legs stretched out, hat pulled over his eyes, enjoying a leisurely nap.

"Jeb," said Amara. She got no response.

"Jeb, wake up," she hissed, sharply tapping the toe of her boot into his shin.

Grabbing his leg, Jeb turned his head up to glare at Amara. "Can't a man git a moment of rest around this place?" he grouched.

"Not when my uncle's paying you good money to be working. Besides, I need to ask you a question."

"Fire away, little lady," said Jeb, not bothering to stand up.

Rolling her eyes, Amara continued. "What did you mean earlier when you talked about not wasting time on that patient?"

"You mean the turncoat Reb?"

Amara's heart sank. That in itself was answer enough.

Jeb keenly eyed Amara up. "Thought I recognized that fellar," he uttered. "Regardless what you high-faluting city folk may think, I ain't stupid. When I heard your little heart-to-heart, I put two and two together. He's the Texan we had in here a few months back. Only then he was a Reb." He rubbed his hands together. "Seems to me you took a likin' to the gent while he was here. Who'd a thunk he'd turn out to be, how'd you phrase that? Oh yeah, 'a low-down, yellow-bellied reptile.'"

Amara grabbed onto the rough wood of the stable to support herself, bracing for what she feared may come next.

"We loyal Southerners, we don't cotton to no traitors. Why, even when times is tight, there's still money to be had turning 'em in."

"What do you intend to do?" Amara asked in a hushed tone.

"Seein' as I stands to make the same whether I bring 'im in dead or alive, thought I'd have a bit 'o fun while earning my reward. Got the word out on the street. 'Bout midnight tonight, there's gonna be a good ol' lynching."

Amara's breath caught in her throat and she shook her head in disbelief.

"You can't be serious."

"Dead serious, little lady."

# Chapter XXIII

Amara departed from Jeb's presence in a controlled walk but, as soon as she rounded the corner, she took off running for the house. Her heart pounded uncontrollably as she made her way from the back of the building to the office. She slammed the door shut soundly behind her and leaned against it as she tried to slow her breathing. When she regained her composure she started pacing the worn Oriental carpet, attempting to get her thoughts together. *Think, Amara, think.* It was hard to even hear her words over the beat echoing through her temples.

She tried to make sense of Jeb's vile words. The mere thought of a lynching was appalling. Amara envisioned Nathan limply swinging from a rope flung over a tree limb. The grisly picture sickened her.

Espionage was punishable by death. Both armies had taken up that practice early in the conflict. Yet, wasn't a man entitled to a fair trial before his sentence was handed down? *Vigilantes don't know what impartial means. Their thirst for blood far outweighs their common sense.* The thought of those despicable men slinking into the hospital gave Amara the shivers.

Perhaps it made the most sense to approach the Union soldiers on guard and tell them what she had heard. They would either believe her or they wouldn't. *Regardless, they would certainly wonder about my distress over the fate of a Union officer.* At this point, even she was beginning to wonder about her distress over his fate. But the thought of any man losing his life because of her impetuous behavior was more than she could bear. *If only I had held my temper in check when I saw him on the operating table, none of this would be happening,* she thought in frustration.

Regaining her focus, Amara evaluated her options. If the officers didn't believe her, such suspicious behavior could lead to repercussions not only for herself but for Doc as well. Plus Jeb would be at liberty to carry out his plan.

On the other hand, if they did think her story was credible, Jeb's objective would be thwarted. That sounded promising but it did bring up two other concerns in Amara's mind.

First of all, Nathan could still be in harm's way. *I don't even know the truth behind his change of colors myself. Maybe he is a spy, but it could just as easily be for the Confederate Army as it is for the Union Army.* She may be putting him in jeopardy with the Union Army and, once again, he would be facing the hangman's rope.

Secondly, if the men accepted her story and transferred Nathan to a safer location, then she would have to deal with Jeb and his cronies. *They'll know who ratted them out and I'll be their next target.* The thought of a coarse rope snapping her slender neck like a dry twig made Amara grab her throat in panic.

If only she had someone to look to for guidance. The one person Amara trusted in the hospital was her uncle, but she did not want to get him involved. *There must be a solution that I can carry out myself.*

Amara sat on the edge of her uncle's hard-backed chair, placed her palms on his desk and forced herself to take a deep breath to clear her thinking. The wheels slowly started to move in her head. First and foremost—Nathan must vacate the property before midnight. There was no question about that.

But how to do that, she really wasn't sure. Alerting the Union soldiers posed too many risks. Asking for Doc's assistance was out of the question. *I cannot drag anyone else into this*, determined Amara. Seeing that the building was under twenty-four hour surveillance, getting an injured soldier out of the hospital without anyone noticing would be a trick.

*A trick?* The wheels picked up speed. *Like when James used to disappear before my eyes when we played hide-and-seek in this very same house?* That was it. Amara rubbed her hands together in anticipation. *All I need to do is to come up with an excuse to get Nathan to accompany me to the attic of the hospital. We can escape through the secret passageway.*

As far as Amara could figure, if she waited until nightfall she would be able to get him off the property without anyone seeing. She knew the streets of Atlanta like the back of her hand—she'd take the darkest, least-traversed route to get Nathan to the McKirnan house. Once they got there, she intended to discern his true colors. If his blood ran blue, she would escort him to the commander's headquarters and then she'd slip back to the hospital before word was out that he was missing.

If he was aligned with the Southern cause, she would take him to Immaculate Conception. She was certain Father O'Reilly would put Nathan up for a few days to complete his convalescence. He had housed plenty of recuperating soldiers in the rectory since the war started— both Confederate and Union men. The priest could then take him to a Confederate outpost. Since Father O'Reilly performed his priestly duties for both armies, he had access to all the camps.

As for herself, her future was harder to map out. It pained her to think about leaving her uncle on his own, but it may be prudent for her to vacate Atlanta temporarily. Any Confederate field hospital would welcome her assistance, she imagined. With his connections, Father O'Reilly should be able to arrange something.

Amara considered the things she would need to gather for her own journey. This would necessitate stealing into her house to pack a bag. Mrs. McKirnan and Theresa were still living there, thanks to Amara's connections at the hospital. Helping them out seemed like a charitable act at the time, now it was coming back to haunt her. But once her items were secured, she and Nathan could be on their way.

The irony of this whole situation was not lost on Amara. She remembered the prayer she had murmured back in the beginning of the summer asking God to bring Nathan back to her. *Of all the prayers in my life God could have answered, He chose that one? Either God has a sense of humor or I'm being punished for something.*

Over the course of the next few hours, she did busywork as she waited for darkness to descend. She sequestered some provisions from the kitchen, bundling the bread, a few hard-boiled eggs, cornmeal muffins and some cured side pork in a napkin. She stowed the food and a candlestick in the alcove next to the stairs that led to the attic.

At the appointed hour, she casually made her way through the ballroom, checking on patients and picking up a few misplaced items. When she neared Nathan's cot, she threw back her shoulders and assumed an air of authority.

"Sergeant Simmons?" she inquired, tapping his left shoulder to rouse him.

His eyes slowly opened as he attempted to focus on the speaker. Recollection of their encounter earlier that day must have come to him.

"You haven't come back to finish the job, have you?"

"Of course not, Sergeant," said Amara in her cheeriest voice. "I'm here to get you up and stretch your legs a bit. We're going to take a little stroll around the building."

When he looked at her skeptically, she hastily added, "Doc's orders."

Nathan eyed her up. "Are you sure you don't intend to walk me to a balcony and push me off?"

For the briefest of moments, Amara looked up to the left as she pondered that intriguing proposal. But she dismissed the thought and continued with her ruse.

"Aren't we the untrusting one," Amara said, clucking her tongue and shaking her head. "We're just going to get you a smidgen of fresh air. Let's fetch your jacket, why don't we? It's a bit chilly this evening."

Although he looked like he still had his doubts, Nathan obeyed and gingerly sat up in the cot. He let Amara tug his coat onto his left arm and throw the other side around the sling covering his right shoulder. Wincing from the pain, Nathan inhaled deeply, let the breath out and pushed himself up to a standing position.

Amara then offered her arm to support him. When he leaned his weight into her she struggled to keep her feet— he was a good head taller than her and as solid as a tree trunk. Planting herself to the floor, she gave him a few seconds to regain his bearings. After determining he was steady on his feet, they took the first step together.

It was a process to make their way across the wooden floor to the double doors. Amara grabbed the doorframe when they were within an arm's length and guided Nathan towards the spot.

"Lean against there a moment and catch your breath. I'll be right back," said Amara, who was in need of a breather herself.

She tiptoed through the doors, looked left and right down the hallway and peeked over the railing to see if anyone was wandering about. All was clear so she scurried to the alcove, grabbed her package and candlestick, and hurriedly lit the candle from a nearby wall sconce.

She stepped closer to the entrance and motioned Nathan to follow her, putting her index finger to her lips to garner his silence.

"Come with me," she whispered when he reached her side.

"Where are we going?" he asked in a hushed voice, matching her tone.

"I'll tell you in a minute. Let's hasten up these stairs before someone observes us."

Nathan gave Amara a questioning look but did as he was told, clamping his jaw shut to keep from wincing in pain as he took the steps one at a time.

When they made it to the landing at the top of the steps, Amara opened the attic door and ushered Nathan in.

"Now can you tell me what you're up to?" asked Nathan, surveying the room with its assortment of furnishings and boxes neatly stacked against the walls.

"Keep your voice low or someone will hear us," scolded Amara. She walked to the window and flattened herself against the wall so she could glance to the street below without being seen. Satisfied with the view, she continued. "I must get you out of here tonight. Your life depends upon it."

"*Really*," he replied skeptically.

"Really. I happen to know that a threat has been directed towards you and it isn't an empty one."

"Exactly what is this threat, who is making it, how do you know about it, and most importantly, why do you care?"

"Good lord, you ask a lot of questions," Amara muttered. Counting on her fingers, she impatiently ticked off the answers. "The threat—lynching. The purveyor of said threat—a Rebel sympathizer. My knowledge—firsthand. My reasoning—I didn't spend an entire afternoon trying to save your godforsaken life just to see it taken away eight hours later."

She walked to the wall on the far side of the space. "Enough questions. Follow me."

Running her hand along the edge of the exposed wood,

Amara found the hidden latch and jiggled it to force the concealed door to swing open. "Be careful on the steps, I would imagine they're thick with dust after being forgotten these many years."

Holding the candlestick above her head, Amara gingerly tested the staircase, cringing when she caught sight of the cobwebs crossing their path. "Jesus, Mary, Joseph," she intoned as she made the Sign of the Cross before starting the downward assent. She watched each step she took, praying she wouldn't encounter vermin of any sort.

The explanation Amara had offered for the escapade they were undertaking was sketchy but, to her surprise, Nathan didn't balk and followed her through the doorway.

"Make sure to shut the door tightly," she instructed from the lower stairs.

He did as she bid and, for the next several minutes, the two descended the circular staircase in silence. A soft screech came from Amara's lips when she ran into an occupied spider web. She could swear she heard chuckling behind her.

"You're more than welcome to lead the way if you think it's so easy," said Amara over her shoulder.

"No, thank you," responded Nathan from the darkness behind her.

When they reached the bottom of the stairs, a sloping tunnel led away from the building. Amara wasn't sure where it surfaced but she prayed they would be able to breach the entrance.

After walking fifty or sixty feet further, they came to the end of the passageway. An ancient door was latched from the inside so it was just a matter of lifting the wooden planking free from its stays to open the portal. Doing so, Amara set the wood aside and stepped over the threshold. Holding the light above her head, she realized they were underneath a massive tree. The roots formed a natural ladder to the ground's surface.

Setting the candlestick down, she climbed to the top and peered through the opening. All she observed was undergrowth, so she squirmed her way out completely and parted the greenery to see where they had landed. Spotting the hospital, she estimated they were in the farthest corner of the property, well away from the street.

She dropped back through the hole. "All is clear." Eyeing Nathan, she continued. "It's going to be a tight fit getting you through the tree trunk. I have to warn you, it may hurt a bit, but we'll be quick about it."

"Tree trunk?"

Amara didn't bother to reply as she snuffed the candle out and scrambled up the makeshift ladder.

She could hear Nathan scaling the tree roots behind her, which she imagined was not an easy task with only one good arm for support. It was a relief to see his head peeking out of the aperture. He paused to inhale the cool night air deep into his lungs.

"Are you sure I can fit through this hole," he asked, as he moved his head up and down, then side to side, checking out the circumference.

"There's no going back, so you're going to have to," said Amara determinedly.

"Push with your feet and I'll pull you from under your arms," she instructed. "Put all your weight on the left so you don't aggravate your wound overly much."

She began to pull as Nathan attempted to get leverage on the roots. Both of their foreheads were glistening with sweat—Amara's from exertion and Nathan's from pain.

"Are you sure this isn't your means of torturing me," asked Nathan as the two slowly inched their way forward.

"Trust me, if I wanted to torture you, I could come up with all sorts of ways that wouldn't require so much effort on my part," whispered Amara as she continued to tug.

The tree finally let go of its hostage and Nathan lay prostrate on the ground, spent from the effort.

"No time for rest. Get to your feet," urged Amara. "We need to make a rapid exit before the alarm sounds that you're missing."

"You're quite the demanding young lady," groused Nathan as he pulled himself up with the aid of a low-hanging branch.

"When it serves my purpose, I can be. Now come along. I'm taking you somewhere safe."

# Chapter XXIV

The two made their way stealthily through the yards with Amara scouting each road they encountered before proceeding across. Gaslight made the main roads too risky to travel so they took a circuitous path to her house. Nathan was on the verge of passing out by the time their destination finally loomed before them.

"We'll let ourselves in the back of the house. My stepsister is sleeping in the bedroom next to the kitchen so we need to be as quiet as possible. But before we go in, I must ask you a question so I can determine my plan of action."

The pale moonlight allowed Amara to look Nathan straight in the eye so she could judge his reaction.

"I've seen you wearing both the blue and the gray. With whom does your allegiance lie?"

"I'm a Northern man born and raised," said Nathan directly. "My loyalty is to the president of the United States and the Union Army. I was..."

Amara put her hand on his mouth to interrupt him before he could go any further. "That's all I need to know." She sized him up as though she had run across a curious species. "I guess that explains the unusual accent."

Nathan looked as if he had more to say but Amara proceeded. "That being the case, I will escort you to the Union command post. You may give the sentry whatever excuse you like for leaving the hospital. I want to make it clear that I acted completely on my own behalf tonight. I would ask your word as a gentleman that you refrain from implicating my uncle in this business."

"You have my word. But what of the Reb who seeks me out?"

That was a good question. Amara didn't want to see any blood spilled because of her; however she was equally leery of letting Jeb and his associates roam the city unchecked.

"If you have some soldiers surround the hospital before midnight, you may be able to catch him red-handed trying to carry out his plans."

She reached for the doorknob. "Go straight through the kitchen to the parlor. You can rest a spell while I pack my valise."

"Where do you intend to go?" asked Nathan.

"Suffice to say, I have a plan," said Amara in a guarded tone.

As quietly as she could, Amara unlatched the door and swept it open. She stepped into the kitchen, looked around and inclined her head towards the parlor. Nathan set off in the proper direction as Amara crept into her bedroom, the sounds of Theresa's heavy breathing filling the small space. If she could make it past Theresa, no one would be the wiser that she had been there. Mrs. McKirnan no doubt was dead to the world, sleeping off the sherry she imbibed of more liberally as of late.

Amara made the Sign of the Cross before tiptoeing to her hope chest. She lifted the cover part way open to reveal her satchel on the top of the stack. She grabbed undergarments, hosiery and a sewing kit. Digging through the trunk in the darkness, her fingertips grazed the soft silk fabric she had received from her father two months earlier. Impulsively she gathered it up and put it on top of the other items. She quietly shut the lid to the chest, straightened up and then pulled two dresses off the pegs on the wall and shoved them in the bag. Thankfully Theresa hadn't so much as stirred one bit. Amara made her way from the room to the front of the house. Nathan sensed her approach and pushed himself up from the Chippendale sofa in the parlor. They had just stepped into the kitchen when the sharp sound of a striking match came to their ears.

Light from the freshly lit kerosene lamp on the kitchen table filtered to the corners of the room. Theresa stepped away from the table, her stepfather's derringer held tightly in her shaking hands. With her starched white nightgown and locks of blond hair streaming to her hips, she had an ethereal appearance.

"Both of you, into the parlor," she stammered.

Amara and Nathan backed up, keeping their eyes on the girl.

"Theresa, put that weapon down. Someone's bound to get hurt," said Amara evenly.

"You're damn right someone's going to get hurt. I'm deciding if it will be my traitorous stepsister or her Union lover," she spat out as she looked between the two.

Amara bristled at the implication. "Theresa, this is not what you think."

Theresa crept forward, backing them further into the room.

"You can just keep your mouth shut, Amara. I know what I see. I just wish your father were here to witness this. You were always the apple of his eye, but I suspected there was rot under that shiny surface. I can't wait to inform Mother that little Miss High-and-Mighty has been fraternizing with the enemy."

"Have you gone mad?" Amara snapped back in frustration. "You would shoot me over some far-fetched accusation you've manufactured in that empty head of yours?"

Theresa clamped her jaw down in anger. "Don't underestimate me, Amara."

She pointed the barrel of the gun from Amara's chest to

Nathan and back to Amara again as she considered her next step.

"Theresa, you can't kill both of us with one shot."

"I know that," she replied testily.

The sound of the clock ticking echoed through the room as Theresa bit her lip and considered the situation, her eyes darting back and forth between the man and woman in front of her.

"Damn it, Amara, you've brought this whole situation upon yourself," she finally said. "I always knew you were jealous of me and all my beaus, but to be so desperate for a man that you would give yourself to a Yankee. It sickens me."

Amara's jaw dropped in disbelief.

"You'll have to live with what you've done, Amara, but I can't say the same for your man."

The girl squared her feet and tightened the grip on the gun.

"It will be easy enough to blame his death on you. This is your father's firearm after all."

Theresa pivoted slightly and trained the piece on Nathan, her eyes livid with anger. "You Yankees have destroyed my life. Before you started this stupid war, I had friends at school, new gowns to wear, parties to attend, and more young men seeking my attention than I could keep track of. Everything is ruined because of you," she said with a catch in her voice. "But after tonight there will be one less filthy Union soldier littering our city. Prepare to meet your maker, Billy Yank."

Amara saw movement out of the corner of her left eye. A body dove towards Theresa just before the gun went off. The blast caught a man in midair and he crashed to the floor. A circle of blood surfaced to the front of his shirt.

Nathan lunged for Theresa and caught her wrists in his left hand as Amara dropped to her knees on the floor.

"James!" she cried out.

She wadded up the bottom of her skirt and pressed it to the wound in an attempt to stem the flow of blood.

"James, hang on. We'll get you to the hospital."

His glazed eyes looked in her direction. "Amara?"

"James, save your strength." She took her right hand and stroked the hair away from his eyes. "You saved our lives, James. You're a hero." He was struggling to breathe but gave her a look of acknowledgment. Amara noticed his eyes starting to roll back in his head.

"Listen to me, James," she said, her voice rising in agitation. "You must hold on. We'll get you help."

James raised his hand to touch his sister's cheek. "No need, Amara," he said in a labored voice. "I'll be back to my old self in no time." He gave her a slight smile and then his head fell to the side, his eyes staring blankly into space.

Tears rolled from Amara's eyes onto James' lifeless body. With a trembling hand, she gently used her index finger to shut each of his eyelids. Amara then turned to Theresa in a fury of rage and grief. "What in God's name have you done?"

Theresa stared at James in horror. The pistol slipped out of her hands. She struggled to get out of Nathan's grasp.

"It was all your doing Amara, you know it."

"You truly are mad. That is a despicable accusation."

Footsteps could be heard coming down the stairs. Nathan instantly took charge of the situation. He shoved Theresa aside and pulled Amara off the floor.

"We must leave," he said sternly.

"But what about James?"

"There's nothing you can do for him now."

He propelled Amara towards the kitchen, grabbing her bag as they went.

Theresa's blood-curdling scream followed them as they exited the house.

# Chapter XXV

By the time they reached the church rectory, Nathan was ghostly pale and Amara was nursing a nasty stitch in her side. That would subside soon enough, but the ache in her chest was a different issue. Her heart was breaking over the loss of her brother.

Amara raced up the steps and pounded on the door.

"Father O'Reilly!" she shouted, keeping a steady beat with both fists. "Father O'Reilly!"

She heard the scrape of a key turning in the lock.

"Ye'll not be accused of having the patience of a saint, by any means," said the mumbling voice from behind the door.

When the door opened a crack, Amara pushed through and stumbled into the foyer. Nathan was but a step behind her.

"Thank God you're here," said Amara in relief.

The priest looked at her blood-stained dress and his eyes widened in alarm.

"Miss Amara, are ye alright, lass?"

Amara grabbed the priest's hands in supplication. "I am in desperate need of your help, sir. My brother James has been shot."

"Dear Lord. Give me a few minutes te gather me things. He will be needin' the Sacrament of the Sick." The pastor started off towards the interior of the church.

"It's too late for that, sir. We've lost him already."

The priest halted mid-stride and turned to Amara.

"'Tis a shame, he was a good man."

"He truly was, sir, and I would certainly appreciate it if you would go to the house in the morning and see to his burial. But we have another matter that needs to be resolved without delay."

"We? Pardon me, sir," said the priest, looking past Amara. "I didn't notice ye standing there. I'm Father Thomas O'Reilly, pastor of Immaculate Conception Church."

"Sergeant Nathan Simmons," said Nathan politely, extending his left hand to the youthful-looking priest. "Nice to make your acquaintance, sir."

"Excuse me, Father," said Amara, pulling the sleeve of his alb. "I don't mean to be rude, but if we could get back to the situation I was addressing." *Bless me, Father, for I have sinned,* she thought as she guiltily dropped her hand from his vestment. "I need a place to stay temporarily until I can find safe passage out of the city. As we speak, my stepsister is probably telling the authorities that James died by my hand. Plus I'm quite certain I've angered a group of Rebel vigilantes. They may already be tracking me down."

The priest raised his eyebrows. "Anything else I should be knowin', lass?"

"Just one other thing—the Union Army might possibly call me to task for abducting one of their officers from my uncle's hospital," rushed Amara, suddenly finding a keen interest in visually inspecting the tips of her kid boots.

It took a few seconds for the good man to absorb what he heard. "It does sound like ye have just reason te be concerned fer yer safety."

Amara looked at him beseechingly.

"But, as much as I would like te help ye, I can't harbor ye here," said the priest firmly.

The color drained from Amara's face. She felt as though the wind had been knocked out of her. "I swear to God, everything I did was done with good intentions. It's not all that it seems."

"I'm sure that's true, lass. But on the morrow twill not

be safe for anyone te remain in Atlanta. I spoke with General Sherman's emissary, Major General Henry Slocum, this very afternoon. Sherman intends te burn this city te the ground. I warned him that desecrating a Catholic church would be a mortal sin. Not only that, it would earn him the wrath of every Catholic soldier in the entire Union Army. I have no doubt he'd have a mutiny on his hands were he te do such a wicked thing. Praise be te God, he took me words to heart and not only is our church to be spared, but the four other churches in Atlanta as well. But fire can be unpredictable. We'll see fer ourselves what's left when the embers die."

"Good Lord, what are we to do?"

"As fer meself, I'm going te do whatever it takes te protect this church. My advice te ye would be te hasten yerselves as far away as possible. Yer best bet is te head west, away from the troubles."

Amara was silent as she considered that suggestion. *Could I depart without seeing James laid to rest properly?* She tucked her hair behind her ears as she thought further. *Where would I go? How would I survive on my own?*

"I have a thought, Father," said Nathan, motioning the reverend aside. "With my arm keeping me out of commission for the time being, I could escort the young lady to my ranch in Texas. We've seen no fighting in our state for more than a year."

"Do ye have kin at yer ranch te look after her?"

"No kin, sir. But I've got hired help. She'll be in good hands."

Father O'Reilly pondered his answer. "Tell me, sergeant, how long have ye known this lass?"

"Miss McKirnan and I first made our acquaintances this past May when I was a patient at her uncle's hospital," Nathan replied.

"Ye get along well enough, do ye?"

"Generally, yes."

"This ranch of yers, be it thrivin'?"

"We've done quite well for ourselves, sir."

"Have ye given thought to a wife and children?"

Nathan looked at him inquisitively. "It is my desire to have both someday, sir," he said sincerely.

Amara's eyes widened at the last exchange and she could no longer hold her tongue.

"Excuse me, gentlemen. I'm not sure where this line of questioning is leading, but if my fate is in the balance, may I enter this conversation?"

Both men turned towards her, expectant looks on their faces.

"While it appears to be a fact that I need to leave Atlanta, who says that I want to traipse halfway across the country to some godforsaken western state or, for that matter, *anywhere* in the company of Sergeant Simmons?" She looked between the two men, her eyebrow cocked.

As though she hadn't spoken, the pair returned to their conversation.

"'Tis very noble of ye offering te bring Amara te yer home state. It seems te me that would be a viable option te ensure the lass' safety. But as a man of the cloth, I cannot condone a young woman traveling unescorted with a man, upstanding as he may be."

The priest clasped his hands behind his back and looked between Nathan and Amara as if to size them up. "These are trying times we're living in now so we can't always do things in the traditional fashion. Sergeant, ye tell me ye want to settle down, correct?"

"Yes, sir," replied Nathan warily.

"Ye've known this lass for the better part of a year. Have ye grown any affection for her?"

The neckline on Nathan's shirt appeared to suddenly feel too snug, as he ran a finger between the collar and his neck as if to give himself more breathing room. He cleared his throat.

"You could say that," he said guardedly, without a glance in Amara's direction.

"I've personally known Amara since my appointment as pastor of this church shortly before the war broke out," said Father O'Reilly. "She's an admirable lass. I think the two of ye would make a fine match."

An audible gasp came from Amara. Nathan and Father O'Reilly riveted their heads to look at her just as her hands flew up to her cheeks.

They both ignored the look of horror on Amara's face and turned back to their conversation.

"This seems te be an equitable solution. But this is not a matter te be taking lightly," the priest said in a stern voice. "If ye feel ye can enter into a sacramental marriage with Miss Amara, I could join ye as husband and wife immediately." He rubbed his hands together in satisfaction and looked to the younger man for his response.

Nathan took in a deep breath and then nodded his head in the affirmative.

Amara's eyes widened at the sight.

"As a married couple, I'll offer ye not only me blessing but me help as well," continued Father O'Reilly. "I'll give ye a mount and see if we can't come up with some funds te help ye along the way."

"Whoa," said Amara, recalling where she had left her voice. She grabbed onto the man's alb once again. *I swear I'll need to start carrying paper and ink to keep track of my sins*, she thought in frustration.

"I must talk to you in private, Father."

He looked at her curiously. "Of course, lass."

She led him to the corner of the room, hoping to be out of Nathan's earshot.

"Father O'Reilly, listen to me. Look very closely at that

man over there." She inclined her head towards the soldier.

The priest did as he was told, scanning Nathan's frame top to bottom.

"Sir, is there anything about him that would cause you to have misgivings about a union between the two of us?"

Looking over at Nathan again, the priest responded. "Other than the damaged wing, he looks te be in good form." Amara rolled her eyes, hoping even God was too busy to notice.

"Oh, I know what ye're after," said the priest, nodding his head. "Sergeant," he called across the room, "do ye profess the Catholic faith?"

"My saintly mother would see it no other way, sir."

"Excellent," said the priest, bobbing his head.

Amara gritted her teeth in exasperation. "Father, look at his clothing."

Nathan was inspected once again. "Well, he's obviously an Army man. No hat covering his head, but other than that, everything seems te be in order."

Quelling her urge to shake the man, Amara ground out three words between clenched teeth. "He's...a...Yankee. Do you see the problem here?"

The priest shook his head, as if admonishing a small child. "Yankee, Confederate, we're all God's children."

The young lady looked anything but convinced.

"Miss Amara, I've always prided meself on my ability to size up a man. Sergeant Simmons is a good one, I know it."

That pronouncement caused Amara to wonder about the man's judgment. *Of course he looks good to you,* she thought, *he looked awfully fine to me when I first met him, too.*

There was no time to go into that, so she went with another tactic.

"Father, he *may* be a good man in your estimation, but

Sergeant Simmons has never once professed his love for me," said Amara, trying to hide the desperation in her voice.

"He cares for ye enough te want te help ye. That's a solid foundation fer any relationship," responded Father O'Reilly. The priest patted Amara's hand. "The love will come in time, my dear."

Having said his piece, the man turned and headed to the sanctuary.

Watching him walk away, Amara put her hands on her hips and whirled around to vent her frustration on Nathan. "Aren't you going to say anything?"

"Why would I? It seems like a sound plan to me. Unless, of course, you have something else in mind." Nathan looked at her expectantly.

Amara's mouth opened but no reply came out. Hearing footsteps returning, her mind clicked into gear.

"It shall be a marriage in name only," she stated. "When we've gotten beyond this situation, we'll go our separate ways."

"Are you suggesting we seek an annulment at some point?"

"Exactly," said Amara, clicking her fingers. "It's the appropriate thing to do. As long as this marriage isn't, um..."

"*Consummated*," supplied Nathan.

"Precisely. Then it will be no sin to terminate it and get on with our lives."

"I'm not so sure of that, Amara. You did hear Father when he mentioned sacramental marriage, did you not?"

"Minor details. As they say, desperate times call for desperate measures."

The priest walked back into the room. "Let's keep this compromise to ourselves," said Amara under her breath to Nathan. "Agreed?"

"Agreed," he replied.

"Time is of the essence now; we need to get on with this," urged Amara. "Shall we proceed?"

Nathan nodded his head and offered his left arm to her.

The couple walked to the altar. Glowing candles softly lit the space. Father O'Reilly stood ready, Bible in hand.

The priest said an abbreviated Mass and switched from Latin to English when it came time to pronounce the vows. After the participants stated "I will," the priest motioned to Nathan who proceeded to cup Amara's chin with his left hand. Bending over her, he placed a chaste kiss upon her forehead. The parish housekeeper, clothed in her dressing gown, signed the official marriage document as witness.

*November 9, 1864, my wedding day,* mused Amara as she read over the certificate before signing in her neat script. It didn't turn out exactly as she had envisioned. As a matter of fact, it didn't turn out anything like she had envisioned. No beautiful silk dress, no veil covering her head, and no loved ones surrounding her. *Not even the groom, unfortunately.* A morose feeling settled upon her.

She joined Father O'Reilly and Nathan in the kitchen as they hastened to make preparations for their departure. The housekeeper added to their stock of food while Father O'Reilly went to his quarters to gather more essentials. He came back with a fistful of gold and silver coins and two sets of clothes.

"Clerical clothing may help ensure your safe passage across the country," he said, handing vestments to Nathan. The man eyed up the cassock, a black hat, the rabat with the Roman collar attached, and the long cape. Without comment, Nathan discarded his military jacket and proceeded to transform his attire.

"We can't very well have a young lady sitting astride a horse with a priest, so we need to change your appearance as well, Amara," said Father. "No one will question the sight of an altar boy riding along with his parish priest to perform God's work. I have garments for you courtesy of a family who lost their son recently. I'm sure they would be glad to see their donations being put to good use."

The clothing was dropped into Amara's arms and she was sent off to a confessional to change before she could utter a word in protest. *Is he serious?* she questioned as she shook out the wool pants, flannel collared shirt and jacket. A pair of work boots and a straw hat completed the outfit.

She made one displeased-looking adolescent male as she stomped back into the rectory, her hair stuffed under the hat.

"Aren't we the fine young gentleman," said Nathan, looking her over facetiously. "Hmm, there's just one thing that needs to be adjusted. I hate to say this, but the name Amara isn't masculine at all. We need to rechristen you for the time being."

He winked at Father O'Reilly. "Thank goodness we've got just the man here to do the job. What shall we call her, I mean him?"

He walked around Amara. "I've got it. How does Amadeus suit you?"

Amara's eyes narrowed.

"Amadeus? Is that the best name you could come up with?" she sputtered. "Do I look like an Amadeus? Do I sound like an Amadeus?"

"'Tis a good Catholic name," noted Father O'Reilly.

"The name came to me because it was similar to your own. But you do have a point about your look and your voice," considered Nathan. "No young man could possibly have a timbre as lovely as yours. I suggest you play the role of a mute on our journey."

"A mute altar boy," said Amara, arms akimbo, a derisive look on her face. *By the time this journey is over, he'll wish I was a mute.*

"And one more thing," Father O'Reilly interjected,

"schoolboys do not possess locks such as yers, Miss Amara. It pains me to say this, but I think they'll need te be shorn. It would be too easy te lose your hat and reveal yer true identity."

Nathan shrugged his good shoulder and nodded his head in agreement.

Amara was sure there were daggers shooting from her eyes—had they been real, there would have been one more casualty added to the Union tolls that day.

"You may want to take charge of this task, Amara," said Nathan as he reached for the shears procured by the priest. "My skills in hair dressing are limited at best, but without my dominant hand available it could get pretty rough."

"I'll do it myself," said Amara angrily. She grabbed the scissors and proceeded to chop her beloved hair close to her head. She was glad no looking glass was in the vicinity. Seeing herself in this state would undoubtedly put her over the edge upon which she precariously teetered.

After finishing the job, she slapped the offending scissors onto the table. She ran her fingers through her hair and instinctively went to tuck a few locks behind her ears. Realizing there was not enough length to tuck, she picked up the straw hat and jammed it on her head.

"Well, that's one way to break a habit," Nathan teased.

Amara didn't give him the satisfaction of acknowledging his words. She grabbed the satchel and headed for the door.

Father O'Reilly escorted the pair to the small barn in the yard and saddled up his horse. It was a sad looking beast and appeared as if it hadn't had a substantial meal in some time. Amara had her doubts whether it could bear the weight of two adults.

"Thank you so much, Father O'Reilly," said Nathan. "I would like to offer you something for the assistance you've given us. If you can make your way to the Union stables tonight, find Lieutenant Jacobs. He's a trustworthy man.

Let him know that I sent you to fetch my horse Kalona. That horse is one of God's finer creatures. She'll serve you well."

"Thank ye for the kind offer," said Father O'Reilly. "I will do that posthaste. We're just hours from the inferno. If I must, I will stable the horse in the church te keep her safe."

"One more thing, Father," added Nathan. "Tell Jacobs to gather several men for surveillance of Doc Burgess' property shortly before midnight."

The priest looked at Nathan in a straightforward manner.

"Son, ye understand that the Union Army will be on me doorstep within no time when ye come up missing, do ye not?"

Nathan held the priest's gaze and nodded his head.

"Ye know, I cannot lie to them when they question me about what went on here tonight."

"I understand that, Father O'Reilly," said Nathan. He pondered the dilemma for a moment and then snapped the fingers on his good side. "Nothing said to you in confession can ever be disclosed, correct?"

"Correct."

"Perfect! I feel the need to confess my sins right now. Amara does as well."

"What?" asked Amara incredulously.

With a look of knowing, Father O'Reilly nodded in consent.

"Let's make our way te the confessional then," he said.

"No time for that," said Nathan hurriedly. "Let's just take care of this right here. I'll start first. Bless me Father for I have sinned..."

In record time Nathan detailed the events of the evening and their plans going forward. When he finished, he elbowed Amara.

"Bless me, Father, for I have sinned," she echoed. "I concur with everything Nathan said to you. Except the part about the cursing. That was only him."

Nathan rolled his eyes before bowing his head for the absolution. Together the couple recited the two Our Fathers and the one Hail Mary they had each been assigned.

With that resolved, the saddle bags were packed and then Father O'Reilly helped Nathan mount the steed.

He then held out his hand to steady Amara as she settled herself in front of Nathan. As overwhelmed as she felt by the events of the evening, Amara was able to gather her thoughts enough to ask Fr. O'Reilly to get word of their situation to Uncle William. She then sincerely thanked the priest for his assistance.

Father O'Reilly accepted her gratitude and placed his hands over the couple in a final blessing. "May the Lord watch over you. Godspeed on your journey." His slap to the rump of the animal sent the pair sailing into the night.

# Chapter XXVI

The horse sprinted a good block before she ran out of steam. *She's got a little more gumption than I gave her credit for*, thought Nathan. With the reins wrapped around his left hand, he directed the animal to a dark alley.

"We need to figure out an escape route that bypasses the checkpoints on the main roads," said Nathan in a hushed voice. "Making our way out unnoticed will not be easy."

"I know the framework of the city fairly well," said Amara. "If you know the whereabouts of the Union troops, I should be able to determine our course."

"Most of the civilians are fleeing west or north so those routes are where the majority of the soldiers are stationed," noted Nathan.

"Then it makes the most sense to head south," said Amara. "We'll stick to the alleyways until we reach the edge of town. Once we're plenty clear of the city, we can pick up the trail to go west."

"That seems logical to me," Nathan agreed. He pulled on the reins to point the horse in the proper direction and nudged his heels into her flanks to get her moving.

They made it to the outskirts of the city without incidence. As they rounded the corner of the last building, they were startled to come upon three soldiers, guns at the ready, who looked like they had been awaiting their appearance.

Nathan pulled the animal up short as a corporal motioned him to halt. *None of these men look familiar but if any of them recognizes me, we're going to have trouble.*

If there was any gunfire exchanged, the whole Union Army would be at their heels.

"Good evenin' te ye, young sirs," said Nathan, his brogue thick as lard on day-old bread. "How can I be of service te ye?"

"Pardon me, Father, but what business do you have riding out at this time of night?" inquired the senior-ranking officer.

"The Lord's business, son. Mrs. O'Halloren be birthin' her tenth child this evenin' and havin' a rough time of it. I've been summoned te administer the Sacrament of the Sick te the missus and her wee one."

The soldiers looked at each other to find a consensus on whether the story was plausible or not.

A stocky private stepped forward. "Why are you with the preacher, kid?"

Amara was silent, her eyes downcast.

"Answer me."

She didn't flinch as he nudged her thigh with the barrel of his gun.

"Ye'll get nothin' from that one, soldier. He's spoken nary a word since he witnessed his family scalped by savages some eight years ago." Nathan paused for effect, looked heavenward and did the Sign of the Cross for good measure. "I've been raisin' him meself and trainin' him in the way of the Lord. God willing, someday he'll find his voice again and follow in me very own footsteps."

One last glance between the men and then the corporal motioned to the south, "You may pass, sir."

"Much obliged. God be with you." Nathan prodded the horse to get it moving again before the men had the chance to change their minds.

When the soldiers were out of sight, Amara whipped herself around. "Follow your footsteps? As you sashay up to the gates of hell? No, thank you." She turned back in the saddle and crossed her arms in front of her.

Nathan stifled his laughter for fear of getting an elbow to the ribcage. He then tugged the bridle to the right, dug his heels into the horse's sides and urged her to gallop as long as she could hold out.

\*\*\*

In the rush to get out of the city, Amara had little time to think about the tragic event she had witnessed earlier that night. Now that they were on the road, the images started flashing before her eyes again. She couldn't believe that James was gone.

No matter how hard it was, she was determined not to cry in front of Nathan. The words her father said to her before he died were still fresh in her mind. *Ye're of sturdy Irish stock. Ye can do anything ye put yer mind te.* The time would come when she would be able to mourn James properly, but until then she vowed she would keep her composure if it killed her. She focused on taking deep breaths and keeping her eyes straight ahead so Nathan wouldn't see her blinking back the tears that threatened to spill over her eyelashes.

Several miles outside the city, they came to a creek. After sliding off the mount and helping Amara down, Nathan picked up a twig and walked to the water's edge and started marking in the sand. The moonlight offered enough light to make the scratching legible.

"Amara, you need to see a map of where we are heading. If something happens to me, I want you to continue on to the ranch."

She looked at him guardedly. "You're not thinking of dying on me, are you?" She stepped close to him, eased his arm out of the sling, and loosened the bandage enough to inspect his wound. The skin around the incision was purplish but no pus was evident and the stitches held fast.

Satisfied with what she saw, she tightened the bandage then tilted her head up to look Nathan squarely in the eye. "I assure you, this is some of my finest needlework. There doesn't appear to be any infection. I predict you shall be as good as new before you know it."

"I have no doubt a more superior piece of stitching has yet to be found, but my arm is the least of my worries right now. We've eight hundred miles to cover before we reach Grayson County. Who's to say what dangers we may encounter as we cross the land? We'll be lucky to cover twenty miles a day with two of us riding this old nag."

Amara's eyes looked up to the left as she calculated the time in her head.

"Forty days? That's nearly six weeks! I haven't even spent six hours on the horse yet and I'm already feeling the ill effects on my posterior," she said crabbily, rubbing her backside. Seeing Nathan looking at her, she dropped her hand to her side and started to pace back and forth in front of the map.

\*\*\*

*Who knows what's going on in that mind of hers?* Nathan could just picture her imagination running wild. *She may still believe I'm a cutthroat mercenary.*

Nathan observed the mixed emotions flitting across Amara's face. She must have come to some acceptable conclusion because she turned her attention towards his etchings. She nodded in comprehension as he explained the roads and landmarks they would encounter.

"It will be safest to stay on the main thoroughfare connecting the five states we will cross," Nathan said. "Alabama has the most difficult terrain with its mountains east of Birmingham."

He pointed to the map. "Jackson is about two thirds of the way through Mississippi so that would be a good spot to replenish supplies. The largest body of water along the route is the Mississippi River which divides its namesake state and Louisiana." A squiggly line represented the river that ran north to south.

"The bridge near Vicksburg may be intact but, if not, flatboats are available for hire. Once you hit Shreveport, it's just a matter of hours before you ride into Texas. Due north of Dallas is Sherman." A star denoted the spot. "Almost anyone there should be able to point you in the direction of my property."

Amara looked intently at the map.

"I'll memorize this," she said as she turned to look at him, "but so help me, if you up and die on me, I will never speak to you again."

Nathan couldn't hold his laughter back.

That apparently didn't sit too well with Amara. She marched to Nathan and stood on her tiptoes to get her face as close to his as she could.

"Don't expect me to light any candles for the repose of your soul, Yankee," she steamed. "You can wander about in Limbo for all of eternity. See if I care."

She lowered her heels to the ground and then stomped to the horse. Grabbing the horn of the saddle, she hoisted herself up. Nathan shook his head at her as he erased the crude map with the heel of his boot. When he was satisfied that no evidence remained, he pulled himself onto the saddle behind Amara.

They set off with a goal of putting as much ground between them and Atlanta as possible before the sun came up. Nathan was at the point of exhaustion and hoped to find a dense forest after first light where they could conceal themselves and the horse for a few hours. Once they were rested, he planned to travel during the day when the roads were safer.

The horse clip-clopped along at an agonizingly slow

pace. Nathan kept alert, scanning their surroundings for signs of trouble. He saw Amara fighting off sleep, but between everything she had been through in the last day and the methodical movement of the horse, she couldn't hold out any longer. With her defense mechanisms down, she leaned into Nathan. He was more than happy to share his warmth and shield her from the chilly autumn air.

\*\*\*

Amara dreamt she was a child again, frolicking with James and Michael. They were playing hide-and-seek and she was searching for them. As time passed and they were nowhere to be found, a feeling of panic overcame her. She shouted their names over and over, racing through a forest, her terror mounting. At last she spotted them on the edge of a cliff. They turned and looked at her, each issuing a nonchalant salute, then shook hands and stepped over the edge together. *No, no, come back*, she pleaded, but they vanished into thin air. She felt like the life had been squeezed out of her. Her breathing became ragged and tears trickled down her cheeks as she stared at the spot where the boys had last stood.

A strong arm tightened around her and she felt herself being gently rocked back and forth.

"Amara, my love, don't fret," someone murmured into her ear.

She didn't know where the voice came from but it soothed her nonetheless. Her fear subsided as she leaned into the warmth and comfort she felt from her protector. From that point on, she slept soundly until the horse slowed to a halt.

Wooly fabric tickled her nose. She inhaled deeply and relished a musky, masculine smell. She let out an unladylike yawn and stretched her arms wide as she slowly opened her eyes. The sight of a white collar tab directly in front of her face brought her awake instantly.

*Jesus, Mary, Joseph, am I in the arms of a priest?* Amara thought in horror. *There aren't enough prayers in the world to atone for this sin.* She snapped her head up, knocking Nathan under the chin in the process. She quickly slipped off the horse's back and stumbled to the ground.

"Well, that's one way to say good morning," Nathan said before moving his jaw back and forth with his good hand to assure everything was still in working order.

"I'm so sorry," Amara blurted out, the color coming to her cheeks.

"For nearly breaking my jaw?"

"Well, that too, but for, um, putting myself in a compromising position with you. I'm not sure what came over me."

"No harm done," Nathan said. He dismounted and busied himself looking through the saddle bag. From Amara's vantage point, it looked like he was hiding a grin.

"We'll have something to eat now and maybe get a few hours of shuteye before we resume our travels. Sound good to you?"

"Yes, thank you," said Amara, still feeling self-conscious.

The two ate their breakfast in silence. Afterwards, they each found a spot under an evergreen tree where they could stretch out on a bed of pine needles and sleep undisturbed. The rest was just what Amara needed to feel refreshed for the next leg of the journey. By noon they were back on the road. Amara sat upright in the saddle, doing her best to avoid leaning against Nathan any more than she had to.

# Chapter XXVII

Over the next few days, they saw numerous other travelers on the road. When Amara noticed people approaching, she pulled her hat low over her brow and cast her eyes down to make herself as inconspicuous as possible. She wasn't sure how well she mimicked a boy and didn't want to raise any suspicions. Nathan tipped his hat to the passersby, but always kept the horse moving forward with a sense of purpose.

Occasionally, a person would ask for a moment of the reverend's time so they could have a blessing or prayer spoken for a loved one. Amara kept silent when Nathan pulled out his best Irish brogue to intone God's benediction on his poor lost sheep. *If he offers to hear someone's confession, I'm drawing the line.*

After the third intercession in less than four hours, Amara was ready to burst. *We will never make it across this state if we stop for every wayward soul.* When the elderly couple was out of sight, she turned in the saddle and shot a look of disdain at Nathan.

"I can see why you made such an effective military agent. Lies roll off your tongue quite easily."

"What is dishonest in offering up a blessing for a distraught child of God?"

"Well, to start, you're impersonating a priest. I would imagine that's at least a venial sin."

"You have a point there. But what would you propose I say to these downtrodden folks?"

Amara considered that for a moment before turning to look straight ahead. "It's your soul, not mine. Say whatever you please."

Nathan shook his head in exasperation.

The pair rode in silence for another hour before Amara blurted out the thought that had nagged her since their last exchange.

"You never denied it."

"Denied what?" Nathan inquired.

"That you were a spy."

"Would you have believed me if I had?"

She shrugged her shoulders and continued to look straight ahead.

After a lengthy pause, Nathan answered. "I am not, nor have I ever been, an emissary for either the North or the South. What say you to that?"

Amara's heart constricted in her chest. She desperately wanted to believe him but didn't want to let on how important his words were to her.

"I would say you need to do some explaining."

"Are you ready to hear the truth?" he asked.

Her shoulders tensed up, she turned her head and shot him a sidelong look.

"I'm ready to listen. Whether or not it will actually be the truth is yet to be determined," she said cagily.

Nathan took in a deep breath and let it out before he started his narration. "This is my truth; it's your decision whether you choose to accept it or not."

"Proceed," said Amara, tilting her chin up.

"I actually had no intention to fight this war for either side, to be honest. Having moved from Illinois to Texas two years before the conflict erupted, I had no allegiance to the South. I was content running my ranch and contributing to the Confederate war effort, albeit somewhat unwillingly, by providing beef to the pillaging troops as they swept through our county."

"You say you had no allegiance to the South, but I saw you wearing their colors when we first met," Amara interjected.

"That is correct. Last spring my business partner Dominic and I were presented with the opportunity to join the Confederate Army."

"And you accepted?"

"We had little choice. The Confederate Army was conscripting new recruits. The pistols they used as calling cards dispelled any thoughts of resistance," said Nathan.

"How is that?"

"It was either join up or be branded Unionists, which in essence was a death sentence in our corner of the world. Dominic and I intended to remain attached to our assigned regiment until we could escape together, either back to Texas or to the Union camps. Our plans went awry during our first encounter with Federal troops. I was injured and transported to Atlanta," Nathan recounted. "It did not go according to my will but a greater force was at work that day."

Amara wasn't sure how to take that statement. *Was he satisfied with the turn of events or displeased?*

"What of Dominic then?"

"I haven't seen him or heard of him since the day I was first wounded," Nathan replied with a note of resignation.

"I'm so sorry," said Amara sincerely.

More questions came to her head but, before she had a chance to formulate them, her attention was caught by sounds coming from the woods bordering the north side of the road. Nathan heard it as well and jerked on the reins to halt the horse.

Two men burst through the brush directly at them. The first man attempted to grab the mare's halter while the other man went after Amara. He seized her arm and unseated her from the horse. She had to do a quick roll to get out from under the thrashing hooves. Nathan had his hands full trying to settle the animal and keep his own seat.

As she attempted to regain her footing, Amara was

yanked back by the collar. She felt the cold edge of a knife against her throat.

"Looks like we's gots us some visitors, Gus," said the younger of the two men, who was dressed in the remnants of a Rebel uniform.

The older man was wearing Confederate-issued brogans on his feet. Obviously, the two were soldiers. But able-bodied soldiers this far away from the battlefront could only mean one thing—they were deserters.

Amara's skin grew clammy as she recalled the tales she had heard of their kind. They roamed the countryside, searching for food and plunder, accosting unaware travelers. Both men looked to be half-starved which indicated the desperate state they were in.

"On behalf of the fine folks of Alabama, we'd like to welcome you to our state," said the man in the butternut trousers, offering an exaggerated bow to Nathan as he stepped back from the horse. "Beggin' yer pardon, padre, but I feel it's my duty to inform you that this here road you'se riding on is a toll road."

"You don't say, now," answered Nathan, looking directly at the man while keeping Amara's captor in his peripheral vision. "What will it take to pass?"

"Seein' as you is a man of the cloth, we won't be askin' much. Just give us what coin you have and you may be on yer way."

Nathan eased himself off the horse and opened the saddle bag. After a show of searching for a few seconds and rattling some coins, he stepped around the back of the horse and quickly raised his pistol in his left hand, aiming it directly at the head of the older assailant. The sound of the trigger being cocked into place caused both men to stand stock still.

"Since when do preachers carry guns?" stammered the man. He pulled Amara closer to the edge of the thoroughfare.

"About the same time Alabama started charging a toll for their roads," Nathan answered. "You—drop your weapon, step away from the youth, and put your hands up."

The man complied, backing closer to his cohort. "Well, if I ain't seen everything," he muttered before spitting some tobacco on the ground.

"Not everything yet," said Nathan. "I want both of you men to get down to your skivvies and pile everything else up over here." He pointed the gun to a spot a few feet off the road.

"Don't see no point in getting' personal here, mister," said the older one.

"Nothing personal at all. I just figured the fewer encumbrances you have the faster you'll be able to run. I'm going to give you thirty seconds to get undressed and hightail it back that away," he said, nodding his head to the east.

Nathan started counting down while the men scurried to remove their clothes. By the time he reached twelve, the men were sprinting away like they had the devil on their heels.

Amara didn't know whether to laugh or cry. She could still feel the spot where the knife had nicked her skin and recall the man's rancid breath on her face. But when Nathan's chuckles turned into full-out laughter she couldn't help but join in. She laughed until she cried and, after a few moments, the laughter turned into sobs. The tears she had been holding in since her brother's death began to flow. Nathan pulled Amara into his arms and let her weep until she had no tears left.

He gave her one last squeeze for reassurance, then started gathering the abandoned garments and stuffing them into the saddle bags to be disposed of later.

She was utterly spent but followed him with her eyes, waiting for him to say something. Amara half-expected some jibe about her soaking his shirt but none was forthcoming.

Nathan assisted her onto the horse and then pulled himself up behind her. As they resumed their journey, Amara was in a pensive mood, trying to sort out who the man behind her truly was.

# Chapter XXVIII

It took more than a week to cross Alabama. Nathan's arm was healing, so he abandoned the sling to make it easier to handle the horse. The weather cooled remarkably as November faded away. One day blended into the next as Nathan and Amara followed the setting sun towards their destination.

The food Father O'Reilly's housekeeper packed for their journey was long gone. While their days were spent plodding ever onward, they devoted their evenings to scavenging through dirt plots for vegetables missed by the field hands. Amara became adept at sneaking around chicken coops in the dark, searching for overlooked eggs.

When they arrived in a city, the first point of business was scouring the general store in hopes of locating some food to purchase. Not one canned good was to be found thanks to the Federal blockade of the Southern ports. The most they could hope for was vegetables and nuts. They stocked up on okra, pecans, beans, corn and peanuts.

It was difficult for Amara to keep up her guise and stay silent when other people were about. She longed to ask for news of the war. But, going from one town to the next, they saw nothing but demoralized faces. In her heart she knew the Confederacy was running out of steam.

The travelers they came across were an assorted bunch. Some appeared to be fugitives like themselves, carting their every worldly possession in wagons or on decrepit donkeys. Older men traversed the route looking to work the fields abandoned by the slaves. Women and children sought out distant relatives after foreclosure notices forced them from their houses. Some people rushed, others appeared to have all the time in the world.

Many a day the couple could travel for mile upon mile seeing nary a living soul. Amara treasured those hours. When they were alone she could talk freely.

The conversations started casually enough with each of them sharing their experiences in the war. Nathan painted such vivid pictures Amara felt she were there alongside him in battle. She couldn't imagine he was being anything less than truthful with her when he recounted those events with such raw emotion.

As she put more consideration into the matter, the probability that Nathan was an undercover agent declined dramatically in her view. When the time was right, that subject needed to be addressed and put behind them once and for all.

*What would it serve him to keep up such a ruse with me*, she pondered one morning a couple days later as the horse continued to plod along. The motion was so familiar to her now she didn't even give it a second thought.

Since the moment they had set out on the journey, Nathan had been nothing but a gentleman. He was intent on seeing her out of harm's way or he most certainly would have discarded her by now. Obviously he had her best interests in mind.

Amara ticked off all the points in Nathan's advantage one by one. She stopped when she ran out of fingers on which to count. Then she proceeded to start the list of flaws in his character that would cause her to distrust him.

When a minute passed and nothing came to mind, she decided to lay her cards on the table.

"Nathan, I have something to ask you," she blurted out.

Her tone must have sounded serious because Nathan pulled the horse to a stop and slid down to the ground. He looked up at Amara expectantly. "Go ahead."

Amara bit her lip, took in a deep breath and said what was on her mind.

"This is the last time I will ask so I want you to tell me God's honest truth."

Nathan jerked his right hand up. "So help me God, I will," he said in a serious tone.

"Are you," she said, looking him directly in the eyes, "or ever have you been," she said as she leaned close to him, "a spy?"

Nathan leaned his head close to Amara, so close she could feel the warmth of his breath on her face.

She waited expectantly.

"No," he whispered.

Their eyes locked and as Nathan held her gaze Amara's heart started to race. She was lost in the moment and her gripped loosened on the horn of the saddle. Before she knew it, she was sliding off the horse and crashed into Nathan's chest, nearly knocking him off his feet.

Amara let out a yelp as she anticipated hitting the ground but Nathan had a secure grip on her. Her right foot was caught in the stirrup and she was dangling precariously from the horse. With one swift motion, Nathan hoisted her back on top of the animal again.

Trying to regain her dignity, Amara adjusted herself in the saddle and addressed Nathan without bothering to look in his direction.

"I forgive you."

"Forgive me," said Nathan incredulously. "So you're the priest now?"

Nathan didn't even bother to cover his laughter as he got up on the horse behind Amara. "What am I going to do with you?" he asked rhetorically, the mirth still evident in his voice.

\*\*\*

With that topic behind them, the dialogue between the two flowed freely. Nathan's life story fascinated Amara. She badgered him for every detail he could recall. A portrait was forming in her mind of his brothers and sisters, his childhood home, his days on the ranch.

While she didn't think it was intriguing by any means, Nathan never seemed to grow tired of hearing about Amara's life either. She told him of her days in boarding school surrounded by the snooty daughters of the plantation owners.

The memories of her mother were dear to her. The woman was an adept storyteller and brought fairytales to life for Amara every night when she was little. As Amara grew up, the tales were of a more serious nature, talking about the hard times her parents and grandparents endured during the Great Famine. The harrowing tale of their escape from their home country and the sorrow her mother felt at leaving her entire family behind never failed to bring a pang of sadness to Amara's heart. She admired both her mother and father for their bravery in leaving everything they had known behind and starting a life in a strange new country. They built a business and a life for their family from nothing.

Amara knew her parents loved her and her brothers equally, but there was something about her that made her exceptional in her parents' eyes, she noted. She was the youngest child, the only daughter and, of greatest significance, she was the first McKirnan to be born on American soil.

Initially Amara was reluctant to talk about Michael and James. The horror of watching James die before her eyes haunted her. Waves of sadness engulfed her when she let her mind revisit that horrendous night. As for Michael, the uncertainty of his fate pained her to no end. It was foolhardy to think she'd ever see him again, dead or alive.

Nathan gently coaxed the subject out of her. Once she knew she could converse on the topic without breaking down, she spoke of them with pride—their service to the Confederate Army, their academic successes, their strong faith.

They weren't perfect by any means, Amara had assured Nathan. Boys would be boys after all, and those two could brew trouble when they put their heads together. They had a reputation in the neighborhood for pulling pranks on the unsuspecting citizens of Atlanta.

One of their favorites was the pin trick. They'd sneak up to a house and take a pin that had a piece of thread tied around it, and secure it between the casing and the glass of an easily accessible window. From a hiding place nearby, they would pull the string and make a tapping noise on the pane of glass. The sound would reverberate throughout the building and the folks inside were perplexed as to where the noise was coming from. The guffaws from the boys usually gave them away, and they made many an escape lickety-split when the irate man of the house came flying out after them.

"Michael was forever picking on James, but if anyone else tried to bully him, they had Michael to answer to," Amara reminisced. "Once, when James was about eleven, he was playing marbles in the alley behind our shop with a couple of boys who had come into town with their father. The two were bragging about their pa, an overseer on a nearby plantation, who had a reputation for brutality with his slaves. James was convinced they were fibbing because no one could possibly treat another human being so poorly. He called them out for being liars, which didn't sit well with them."

She continued on, the memory getting more vivid as she went. "The pair jumped James and started pummeling him. I was frightened out of my wits and couldn't move.

The next thing I knew, Michael came racing around the corner of the house and barreled into one boy, knocking him to the ground. Then he turned on the other. The first fellow got up and grabbed his brother by his suspender strap, and they scrambled out of the alley like the cockroaches they were. The last I saw them they were cowering under their father's wagon in the street."

Nathan chuckled. "That sounds like me and my brothers. We were constantly getting into brawls. Lord help us if my father was nearby. If he saw two of us going at it, he'd grab each one of us by the back of our shirt collars and smack our heads together. I guess it was his way of knocking a little sense into us." Nathan rubbed the top of his head. "I wouldn't be surprised if I didn't still have a knot or two up there."

The more they talked, the more tales Amara recalled. Conversing with Nathan was just the medicine she needed to help ease the incredible sorrow she felt about her brother's death. The timbre of Nathan's voice was soothing and his stories revealed the man he really was—one who grew dearer to her each day.

\*\*\*

As they crossed the state of Mississippi, the remains of autumn clung to the countless trees they passed. Leaves in faded shades of gold and crimson dangled for their lives from the barren branches. The evergreens stood tall and dotted the landscape with their steady color. A person could barely tell the state had been ravaged by war.

The horse's gait had a rhythmical sound and songs started running through Nathan's mind as they went along. Apparently it was the same for Amara as well, as he caught her humming a tune under her breath one bright morning.

"Amara, if I'm not mistaken, that sounds like a church

hymn. You wouldn't happen to know the words, would you?"

"Well, as a matter of fact, I do," she replied. "We may not be allowed to sing hymns during Mass but, as far as I know, there are no rules that say women can't memorize them."

"I haven't heard that sung in as long as I can remember," said Nathan. He craned his neck to the left to catch her eye. "Would you mind indulging me a bit and singing a couple of verses?"

Amara did not make eye contact with him, but Nathan could see the color rising in her cheeks.

"If you can't, that's fine," said Nathan, throwing down a challenge he sensed Amara wouldn't be able to resist.

He could feel Amara straightening up in the saddle and then the words poured out. Nathan listened to the song, savoring every note. *Her voice is even sweeter than I remembered.* He had to give her credit for performing for him after the teasing he had bestowed on her at the hospital.

With her guard now dropped, songs freely flowed from her. Singing made the time pass quicker and became a part of their daily ritual. When the roads were clear, Amara sang ballads from her father's native land, church hymns or popular ditties she had picked up from the soldiers in the hospital. If Nathan was familiar with the tune, he would join in. Their mix of soprano and tenor voices made a melodious sound.

The more miles passed, the deeper their conversations went.

"Did you ever picture your future life?" Nathan inquired one rainy afternoon.

"My future life? What girl wouldn't?" Amara replied, pulling a blanket tighter around her shoulders to ward off the chilly breeze.

"What does a young miss growing up in Atlanta dream of?"

"Well," said Amara, as she considered the question, "my first plan was to graduate with honors from the Lucy Cobb Institute and show those other girls a thing or two. Of course, that idea was quashed when I was unceremoniously given the boot so Theresa could take my position."

*We've got another thing in common*, thought Nathan, recalling the day his father ended his formal education.

"Were you upset when a stepsister was added to your family?" he felt compelled to ask.

"I was probably more upset being gifted with a stepmother before we had even finished mourning our own mother's passing. But my father was devastated by her death. Perhaps Mrs. McKirnan saved his heart from giving out even earlier than it did. Who is to say? As far as Theresa goes, I thought having a sister was exciting at first. But it didn't take me long to see that she and I were anything but kindred spirits."

"I assume you didn't give up on your dreams completely?"

"Just altered them, is all. I went to sleep most nights picturing my knight in shining armor, galloping up to our store and sweeping me into his arms. He would be so handsome, Theresa's hair would turn green with envy," Amara said with a laugh. "We would ride into the sunset until we reached the castle he had built for me with his bare hands. Our days were spent working side by side. He would use his brute strength to fend off our enemies, and I would employ my keen logic to build our fortune. We would be blessed with two boys who were as handsome as their father and two little girls who were as sweet and adorable as...me!"

It was Nathan's turn to laugh. He admired her indomitable spirit. "You've left nothing to chance, I see."

"I needed something to hang onto in my most desolate moments. What of your expectations for life?"

"My dream," Nathan said reflectively, "I believed I was living it." Pictures of his land and the ranch and the people he left behind came to him. He paused a few moments before proceeding. "I had the earth beneath my feet, the stars over my head, close friends nearby and I made an honest living. I had," he paused, "just about everything a man could ask for."

Amara was silent at that point, leaving Nathan to wonder what she thought of the life he had described for her.

They continued along, with the sound of the rain bouncing off slick leaves and the horse's hooves breaking the suction of the mud the only accompaniment to their thoughts.

Their reverie broke when Amara cleared her throat to get Nathan's attention.

"Yes..." said Nathan expectantly.

"Father O'Reilly says it's easier for a camel to go through the eye of a needle than for a rich man to get into the kingdom of heaven," said Amara with a tinge of guilt in her voice. "So I don't want you to misconstrue my intentions when I talked before of obtaining wealth."

She caught him off guard with that statement. It was actually the last thing he was thinking but he couldn't help but play her for a bit.

"Misconstrue? Not at all. Why wouldn't you want to be rich? New gowns right and left, jewels for every finger, servants waiting on you hand and foot. I can just picture it now," Nathan said in a regal fashion.

"That isn't me and you know it," said Amara indignantly. "I don't want money for myself. I dreamed of building a hospital and a school. With all the widows this conflict has created, women will need to have a means of supporting their families."

"Really now," said Nathan, adding a note of skepticism to his voice.

"And I want to build a church," Amara rushed on. "A grand one with stained glass windows and a marble baptismal font and a pew near the front with the family name on it. And in my grandest imaginings, I see my very own son behind the altar consecrating the bread and wine. He'll make one fine priest, I just know it."

"Of course, why wouldn't he, if he takes after his pious mother!" The note of amusement in Nathan's voice made Amara turn to look at him.

"Are you teasing me again?" His smug look was enough to confirm her suspicions. "You'll be darn lucky if I allow a heathen like you mop the floors in my new church, let alone worship there."

Amara could feel Nathan's shoulders shaking as he tried to suppress his laughter.

"Men, humph!"

He couldn't stop himself and his laughter rang out through the trees. *What a girl!*

# Chapter XXIX

Vicksburg had seen its share of fighting before succumbing to Union forces, coincidentally enough, on Independence Day the previous year. Amara was interested to see the city, having heard about the forty-seven day siege Major General Ulysses Grant orchestrated to capture the city and, ultimately, control of the Mississippi River. Except for the U.S. flags prominently displayed on civic buildings and a few roaming Union patrols, the city looked like most of the larger municipalities they had passed through so far.

One remarkable thing about the location was the abundance of food stocks available for purchase. Nathan and Amara bought a dozen canned goods; enough, they estimated, to tide them over for the last two weeks of their trip.

The bluffs lining the mighty Mississippi offered a spectacular view of Louisiana, the last state they needed to traverse before reaching Texas. Standing next to Nathan, Amara could feel his sense of anticipation. She was happy for him that he would be returning to the life he loved, but wondered how she would fit in there. *Like all things, only time will tell.*

The bridge was under repair so they hired a rickety flatboat to ferry them across the river. Amara clung to Nathan's arm and kept her eyes fixed on the far shore. Never having had the opportunity to learn to swim, the thought of being dumped into the turbulent river frightened her half to death. The craft bounced and jolted with every movement of the water below them. When a steamboat crossed their path Amara screeched and threw her arms around Nathan, burying her head into his chest. The craft's proprietor gave her a strange look.

"He only screeches when he's frightened," said Nathan to the man, who gave Amara a second look before turning back to his work. A heel stomped on the top of his foot brought out a yelp from Nathan. The man snapped around.

"Apparently I do too."

The boat operator moved to the opposite side of the craft, putting as much space between him and the twosome as possible.

Amara was happy to disembark from the contraption on the far side of the river and return to solid ground. She wasn't looking forward to mounting the horse once more. It would take a good nine days to reach the Texas border. When the horse was watered, she reluctantly put her foot in the stirrup. Nathan pulled himself up behind her with ease.

The animal plodded west once again. As they proceeded along, Amara was enchanted by the beauty surrounding them. The terrain alternated between gentle hills, hardwood swamps, bayous and cypress forests. Wildlife was in abundance including deer, geese and the occasional alligator poking its head up from its swampy hideout. The reptiles gave Amara the shivers and she was glad to be on horseback, as bone jarring as it was.

The sight of bald eagles flying overhead made Amara yearn for the freedom to soar into the clouds and leave all her problems and sorrows behind her. Somehow their presence reassured her that the whole world wasn't completely topsy-turvy and gave her hope that the country would be at peace again someday.

One particular eagle caught Amara's attention when they were within a day's ride of the Texas border. It was nearing dusk when the majestic bird first caught their eyes. It lazily circled above them, disappeared from view and then reappeared. Nathan and Amara both thought that was the last they would see of it but it came back again and again, always heading towards the horizon.

"He seems to be intent on following us, does he not?" questioned Amara.

"Leading us, to be more precise," replied Nathan. "If I didn't know any better, I would say the fellow is showing us the way home."

"I'll take that as a good sign," said Amara. She made the Sign of the Cross and silently thanked the Lord for His protection thus far on their journey. For another hour she continued to watch the bird in flight, until the dusk hid him from view. Within a few minutes, Nathan pulled the horse to a stop.

"We'll rest here for the night," he said, slipping off the horse and then reaching for Amara.

Looking around, Amara had an uneasy feeling. They had dismounted much too close to a swamp for her liking. She stayed near Nathan as he unpacked their gear. He scrounged around for kindling to start a campfire. Once he had enough secured he struck a match and set the pile aflame.

"Tend the fire for a few minutes, Amara. I'm going to see if I can't find us a rabbit or squirrel for dinner." He dug his pistol out of the saddlebag and started walking away from their encampment. He glanced back, and noticing her worried look, he reassured her. "I won't be far. If you need anything, just call out. I'll hear you."

Amara put on a brave face but felt less than courageous. She grabbed the saddle blanket off the horse, and wrapped herself up before crouching down to add more fuel to the blaze. She was bone weary and the dancing flames were mesmerizing, yet every creak and stirring she heard caused her to jump. *Amara, don't be such a scaredy-cat,* she chided herself.

When a soft padding sound came up behind her, she turned with relief to greet Nathan. That feeling was short-lived when she realized the man approaching her did not match Nathan's stature. She stood up, threw the blanket aside and positioned herself behind the fire to put space between herself and the intruder. A sense of trepidation turned to fear when the man stepped into the light of the fire.

"Jeb," she croaked, alarm clearly written on her face.

"Long time no see, Miz Amara. Or is that Master Amara?" Jeb snorted, observing her outfit. "You ain't foolin' no one with that there get up. I knew it were y'all a mile away."

"You've been following us?"

"Trackin' ya be more like it. Didn't help that y'all got a big head start. Spent a lil' time in the pokey, thanks to you, missy," he said in a bitter voice. "Them Union boys ain't the friendliest of jail keepers, if'n ya knows what I mean. Got me the stripes to prove it. You're a medical person, I'm sure you'd appreciate their handiwork. Wanna take a look see?"

Amara shook her head from side to side as she backed up a step.

It was obvious the vigilante's plot had been foiled. The man was clearly set on revenge. Amara needed to buy some time because she knew Nathan couldn't be that far away.

"They let you go free then, after all that?" she queried, somewhat louder than she needed to, hoping Nathan was within hearing range.

"That's one way to look at it. Had me a little time to do some craftin' while I was in solitary confinement. The private they had guardin' me didn't voice no objections to me skippin' out once his throat was slit."

Amara's face grew two shades paler. *Good Lord, the*

*man is a murderous lunatic. Where in God's name is Nathan?*

Her fear must have been evident because a look of satisfaction came to Jeb.

"Bet ya'll wondering what brings me out to this here neck of the woods, huh?" He hooked his thumbs in his suspenders and puffed up his chest.

Since he had gone to all the trouble to track them down, Amara had a pretty good idea, but she wanted to keep the conversation running to buy more time.

"That question has crossed my mind," she replied.

"Course ya'll can figure I weren't none too happy with a particular lady after she ratted me out to the Union Army. Used to lay awake at night in my cell figuring out ways to repay her for that little deed. I can actually get pretty creative when I put my mind to it. Most of the ways involved a bit of pleasure for me, some pain for her. But what's the sweet without the sour?"

A look of revulsion came to Amara's face and she took another step back.

"Figured after I was done with her, she wouldn't be lookin' down her purty little nose at this fella anymore. Once I broke her I'd leave her bones at the side of some lonely road for the vultures to pick at."

The intensity of Amara's distress raised dramatically.

"Course, all that was before I busted loose and saw me the posters hung round town. Looks like I gots to keep her alive for the time bein'."

Amara wasn't sure what he meant by those words. Her confusion was apparent.

"What, you ain't heard?" asked Jeb with feigned surprise. "Seems like that same young lady gots herself in a heap o' trouble. Uncle Sam's got a price on her head. Two thousand U.S. dollars for the capture of the Miss that done kidnapped a Union sergeant."

Amara found her voice once again and snapped at Jeb.

"It was not a kidnapping and you know it. I rescued him from you and your mob."

"Don't matter what I knows. Only matters what I's gonna git for turnin' y'all in. Who's gonna believe Miz Amara, 'specially after I tells everyone about the conversation I had privy to between you and the Yank. Sounded to me like y'all was threatenin' the man. If he were to be found pushin' up daisies, all fingers be pointin' yer way, far as I can tell."

The implications of his words sank in and Amara quickly took in a deep breath and started scanning the area around her to make her getaway. Interpreting her actions, Jeb pulled out a Union pistol from the back waistband of his trousers and pointed it directly at her heart. "I wouldn't do that if'n I was you."

Amara released her breath in frustration. Her mind raced as she considered her predicament. As much as she longed to see Nathan at this very moment, his life would be in jeopardy if he walked into Jeb's snare. She decided to keep the man talking so she could keep thinking.

"What made you think Nathan was in my company?" she asked.

"Didn't take much figurin'," said Jeb with a swagger to his voice. "When the sarge come up missin' from the hospital, I knew you musta had a hand in it. I seen the way you eyeball'd him up when youse thought no one were watchin' you."

Amara could feel her cheeks flushing.

"How did you track us down?"

Figured if'n that were the case, the two of you'd be scuttlin' off that a way. There ain't but one straight route run from Georgia west. If I got me a nice piece of horse flesh, guessed I'd catch up with y'all sooner or later. Noticed the preacher man had him one dandy lookin' filly. He was more'n happy to let me take her off his hands."

"Tell me you didn't hurt Father O'Reilly," said Amara, the concern evident in her voice.

"Just gave him a lil' tap with a shovel. He took hisself a nice nap, probably woke up with a goose egg. I'm sure he was preachin' up brimstone and hellfire by the next service."

Relief washed over Amara, but she still needed more time to formulate a plan. "You stole the reverend's horse, but how can a man in your condition travel so far at such a rapid speed?"

"You talkin' about my war wounds and this wicked limp I'm sportin'? Lookie here. I can walk like the best of 'em now," Jeb said, strutting in a quick circle.

"You weren't sick? You weren't injured?" Amara asked in astonishment.

"Well, I was sick alrighty. Sick of getting' my hinder shot at by the Union troops. Figured I'd do me a little actin' and get out while the gettin' was good."

Amara had to bite her tongue to refrain from telling him what she thought of two-faced cowards. Her mind raced.

"Fine. I surrender," she nearly shouted. "If you feel you must escort me back to Atlanta, so be it. We'll leave immediately."

"Not so doggone fast, little lady. I has some business to attend to first. Where's yer man?"

Amara carefully considered what to tell him. "He's off looking for game. He went that direction," she said nodding her head towards the path Nathan had set out on.

"Didn't I tell y'all before that I ain't stupid?" said Jeb, as he slowly made his way around the fire to get closer to Amara. "He may be out huntin' but I don't believe y'all is tellin' me the truth about the direction he set off in." He lunged at Amara and grabbed her left arm in a steely grip.

"Hows about we set off this-a-way? he said, nodding to the opposite side of the clearing. He pushed the barrel of the cocked gun under her chin and backed away from the fire, surveying the woods as they went.

"Got me some nice bait to catch me a big ol' possum." He took another step back. Amara was tempted to dig her boot heels into the dirt to keep him from dragging her away from the light of the fire, but the gun pressed into her neck made her think better of that.

"Mr. Union Man," called Jeb. "Come out, come out, wherever y'all is." The words ricocheted off the trees and faded away. Save for the sound of an owl hooting a distance off, there was no response.

Jeb raised his voice. "Got somethin' of y'alls, Sarge." He pulled the gun away from her neck and recocked it. The sound of metal hitting metal rang in Amara's ears.

Still nothing. Amara could sense Jeb's nerves starting to rise. He looked at their shadows being cast by the fire and retreated several more steps so they were completely enveloped by the darkness.

Panic rose in Amara's chest as she realized they were close to the edge of the swamp. She didn't relish being shot, but drowning didn't sound that appealing to her either.

Her breathing was shallow as she waited. Jeb had his hand locked onto her arm as he looked all around him, watching for Nathan to appear. The intensity of the situation heightened Amara's senses. Every slight movement from the trees caught her attention. The smell of damp moss hung in the air. She could even hear the quiet sound of something slipping through the water behind her.

She began to visualize a water moccasin slithering across the surface of the murky water, ready to sink its fangs into her leg. *How many more ways could I possibly die tonight?* she questioned morbidly. Her nerves were making her imagination run wild, but she just had to look to be sure it wasn't a snake honing in on them. As discreetly as possible, she turned her head to the right and cast her eyes down towards the water.

Good God, it was worse than she could have ever thought. Like a goblin rising from the grave, an alligator slowly came up behind them. A scream escaped from Amara's lips and, in a flash, the beast had its jaws wrapped around Jeb's leg. Jeb shrieked in pain and turned his gun on the assailant while still keeping his grip on Amara. A shot grazed off the beast's armored back. The infuriated animal snapped his head back and forth, pulling both his prey into the water. Amara had a chance to take a quick breath before she and Jeb were completely submersed.

Utter panic set in. Amara could feel her body being pulled further under. She had to get Jeb to let go of her. She tried swatting at his hand but the water made her blows ineffective. Her next point of attack was using her nails to dig into his skin. He loosened his grip but, as she tried to get away, he caught her wrist and hung on as though she were his lifeline.

She was running out of air and ideas. In a last desperate attempt, she reverted to the weapon her brothers knew well from their childhood. She bit Jeb's hand so hard she broke through the skin. His hand went limp and she managed to get free. She put a precious few inches between them so she'd be out of his reach.

By this time, she was so exhausted she could barely move her arms, but she knew she had to get to shore. She flailed away and finally broke the surface of the water and got some air into her lungs. A hand reached out and grabbed her shirt sleeve and she was pulled completely onto the dirt.

Both she and Nathan witnessed the death roll the alligator executed on its victim. Even if they had been of a mind to attempt it, there was no saving Jeb. Nathan put one arm around Amara's shoulders, grabbed her under her knees with his other hand and lifted her off the ground to get her away from the swamp.

Amara began to cough, trying to dislodge the swamp water from her lungs. It took her several minutes before her voice and energy came back to her. She then started to wriggle to get out of Nathan's arms.

"Where in God's name were you?" she sputtered, breaking free from him. "Didn't you see that dog had a gun pointed at my head?"

"I was well aware of that fact. I was biding my time, ready to make a move when the opportune moment presented itself."

"Would that have been before or after I was shot, drowned or eaten by an alligator?"

"It would have never come to that. I had everything under control."

"Under control, my foot." Amara stomped over to the fire and started kicking dirt over the flames. "Next time why don't we let you go for a swim in alligator-infested waters with a madman who has a gun stuck in your neck, and I'll watch from the safety of the trees," she screeched.

"Would you promise to save me?" asked Nathan sweetly.

"Oh, everything would be under control, trust me," said Amara sarcastically.

"Let me think on that," said Nathan with a laugh. He adjusted the packs on the horse and then offered to help Amara up.

She slapped at his hand and mounted unassisted. Easing himself up behind her, he couldn't help but lean towards her and ask, "Were you really eyeballin' me up?"

"The only one who's going to be eyeballin' you up is that gator when you fall off this horse," said Amara irritably. She dug her heels into the horse's flanks and the surprised animal shot off, causing Nathan to tighten his grip on her waist to keep his seat.

"You're not going to lose me that easily, Miz Amara."

# Chapter XXX

The horse hadn't galloped more than one hundred feet when Nathan pulled on the reins to bring it to a standstill.

"Aren't we forgetting something?" he asked Amara.

"If you mean forgetting about watching a man become alligator bait and hightailing it out of this swamp posthaste, I'd say no," replied Amara, repositioning herself after nearly being thrown from the saddle.

"I'm talking about Jeb's reference to his means of transportation. Kalona is out here somewhere. I'm not leaving until we find her."

Nathan dismounted without waiting for a response and tied their nag to a tree. Amara was close at his heels. Without delay he started calling out for the horse.

"Kalona, are you out there girl? Kalona!"

Hearing only the crickets chirping, Nathan put his thumb and forefinger to his lips and let out a shrill whistle and then waited again. Still there was no answer. They made their way further up the road and he repeated the call. A faint whinnying was heard through the brush. The sound grew louder as they retraced their steps. Finally they spotted the creature. Nathan approached her, hand outstretched. When Kalona nuzzled his palm, he put his arms around her neck.

"I didn't think we'd meet again in this lifetime, girl," he said with a catch in his voice. He continued to hold her. *Thank you, God, for bringing her back to me.*

He could hear Amara swallowing a lump in her throat and he stood back to make proper introductions.

"Kalona, this is Amara. Amara, this is Kalona," said Nathan politely. "I'm sure you two ladies will get along just fine."

Amara stepped towards the horse and stroked Kalona's head.

"Hello, girl."

The horse nodded its head as if acknowledging the new acquaintance.

"Guess we're both going to be getting a new home soon."

She leaned in and using a stage whisper, spoke into the horse's ear. "You've been through hell and back with Nathan. Is he truly as decent a man as he appears to be?"

The horse raised and lowered its head as if answering in the affirmative. Amara couldn't help but laugh.

"You've either got her well-trained or she's got a knack for evaluating humans."

Nathan untied the animal from the tree where it had been tethered.

"The latter, of course," he declared in mock seriousness.

"Well, ladies," announced Nathan, "we should get back on course. We'd be mighty obliged, Miss Kalona, if you'd take the two of us."

With no complaints issued from the mare, Nathan helped Amara into the saddle. He walked back to the other horse and grabbed its reins before seating himself behind Amara.

"When we get to Shreveport tomorrow, we'll trade the reverend's horse for some other provisions to complete our voyage."

Nathan wasn't sure who in their right mind would trade anything of value for the decrepit animal. They may have had their share of complaints about the beast, but it did take them a quarter of the way across the continent. That was yet another sign of God's blessings on their journey.

When they arrived in Shreveport, disposing of the animal was easy enough. A shopkeeper gave them a scant few canned goods in exchange for it. *He probably got the better end of the bargain,* considered Nathan. Of course, the worst end of the deal may have been for the horse. Looking at the man's bone-thin children, Amara and Nathan weren't completely convinced the animal wasn't going to be the guest of honor at Sunday dinner.

The two decided to put that thought behind them and concentrate on the final leg of their journey.

Riding Kalona, they increased their speed nearly twofold. The prairie land of northern Texas was easier to cross than the other terrain they encountered on their way.

"At this rate, we should be in Grayson County in three days," noted Nathan.

"Praise God," replied Amara earnestly. December was nearly half over and it was starting to get downright cold.

"I'll agree with you on that," said Nathan.

His thoughts turned to the ranch. "I can't help but wonder about everyone we left behind. Hopefully the men harvested enough crops to stock the food cellar and chopped plenty of wood to keep the fires going until spring."

The sense of anticipation they shared was palpable. Even the horse seemed to notice the excitement and grew more restless at each stop.

The last night on the road, neither Nathan nor Amara could sleep so they decided to press on. After the horse had adequate time to regain its strength, they went forth. The sun was just coming up behind them on an unseasonably mild day as they ascended a ridge on the fringe of Nathan's property.

This was the moment he had been praying for since the day he and Dominic had been escorted off the ranch.

"Are you ready to see the homestead?" he asked, slowing the horse down.

"I've been ready for weeks. I'm anxious to see if the picture I've painted in my mind matches reality," she replied enthusiastically.

"Hopefully you won't be disappointed with what you see," said Nathan in a concerned tone. "This ranch means the world to me. I have a tendency to oversell it."

Nathan nudged the reins to set the animal in motion again. He positioned himself in the saddle to catch Amara's initial reaction. For some reason it was of the utmost importance to him that she be pleased.

When they came over the embankment, Amara's hands flew to cover her mouth.

Looking over the land, Nathan tried seeing it through Amara's eyes to judge if the shock he saw on her face boded well or ill.

The scene was actually quite picturesque, if he did say so himself. A cow lazily grazed, horses trotted in a pen near a stable, chickens bobbed for grain. The centerpiece of the image was the quaint house and the two smaller buildings behind it.

Smoke curled from the chimneys of all three structures and the promise of a warm fire, a home-cooked meal and a soft bed was nothing less than enticing.

Amara turned in the saddle and shot Nathan a look of appreciation and happiness that made his heart soar. It conveyed more to him than any words could ever say. A smile lit his face. He tightened his grip around her waist.

From their vantage point, they could see two men deep in discussion in the yard. The men turned in their direction when they heard the horse's hooves slapping the hard ground. Instinctively, the duo straightened their gun belts with one hand as they shaded their eyes with the other to determine who their visitors might be. A dog came rushing from behind the house to inspect the newcomers and circled the horse, barking in excitement.

As they drew up to the men, the two recognized Nathan and smiles crossed their weathered faces. They then turned their focus to Amara and looked as startled to see her as she was to see them. Her eyes widened. Noticing her reaction, Nathan realized he had forgotten to tell her a few details about his hired men. She was probably wondering why there was a Negro and an Indian on the ranch, both armed.

The color of their skin was inconsequential to him but she may have some concern. *She'll get over it*, he reasoned. Personally he was so glad to see them, he could not have cared less if their skin was polka-dotted.

Amara turned her head towards Nathan, presumably to see his reaction. He was grinning from ear to ear.

"Well, look at you, Nathan," said the black man, shaking his head in wonder. "We was under the impression they was recruitin' for the military, not the seminary."

Nathan had forgotten about the clerical garb he was wearing.

"It's tough times for everyone, Ol' Joe," he replied with a laugh. He dismounted and helped Amara down. She took a step behind him. Nathan went to stretch his hand out to the Indian, but the man immediately pulled him into an embrace.

"Praise the Great Spirit you have returned. My head tried to convince me that I would never see you again, but my heart knew."

"Snapping Turtle, the heart always wins, does it not?"

Ol' Joe stepped forward and threw his arms around the much younger man in a bear hug. "You had Maria worried sick. She done near wore that rosary of hers down to nothin' praying for you every day."

Amara was hanging behind, looking as if she didn't want to intrude on the men's reunion.

"What'd you bring with you?" asked Ol' Joe, stepping past Nathan.

"Not what, but whom," corrected Nathan. "Ol' Joe, Snapping Turtle, this is Amara."

Taking a step closer, Ol' Joe squinted his aged eyes.

"Amara? He's a she?" Amara self-consciously took off her hat and ran her hand through her hair.

"Absolutely. Don't let her looks right now fool you. She cleans up just fine." The remark earned Nathan a glare from the only blue eyes in the bunch.

"Don't matter what she looks like," said Ol' Joe. "I's just glad you's got yerself a lady. Them preacher duds caught me off guard. Don't think I could handle working for a man of the cloth. I can only be on my best behavior so long before I goes back to my normal ways."

The comment elicited laughter from the other two men.

The dog prancing around their feet finally caught Nathan's attention. "Hey, Checkers." He bent down and scratched the canine's ears and was rewarded with exuberant kisses. "I guess you missed me too."

Two more people came tumbling out of the house—a stout older man with a plump woman trotting right behind. They were both short of breath by the time they reached the group. The woman raised her arms in praise, chanting "Santa Maria, Santa Maria." Tears rolled down her cheeks. Nathan gathered the man and woman in his arms at one time and started speaking to them rapidly in Spanish. The woman nodded her head as he spoke and the tears continued to fall.

"Amara, this is Eduardo, who works on the ranch, and his wife Maria, our housekeeper and cook."

"Did you say cook?" Amara clapped her hands in delight. "I am so glad to meet you," she exclaimed. "You will never know how glad."

The woman had a confused look on her face but gave Amara a slight curtsey.

All at once everyone started talking, bombarding Nathan with questions about the experiences he had undergone since they were last together.

***

Maria eventually was able to shoo everyone into the house. When Amara stepped through the door, the smell of bacon frying made her stomach start to grumble. She was embarrassed that someone may have heard the unladylike sound. Maria smiled and timidly motioned her towards the dining room. The wide plank wooden floors shone and windows running along two walls were decked with starched blue calico curtains. Dried wildflowers were arranged in a vase on the long wooden table. A hearth made of fieldstones outlined the fireplace and the brightly burning fire within. Maria pulled out a chair from the table and indicated that Amara should be seated.

The lady scurried off and moments later was back with a heaping platter of biscuits, a bowl of gravy, mounds of bacon and a kettle of grits. The aroma of the food brought the men to the table and everyone hastily sat down. The males looked ready to devour the food they had dished onto their plates, but waited eagerly for Amara to go first. Amara in turn looked at Nathan expectantly.

"You're going to lead us in grace, are you not?"

"Grace? Of course." Nathan removed his hat and waited while the other men followed suit. He cleared his throat. "In the name of the Father and the Son and the Holy Ghost. Bless us, Oh Lord..."

Amara bent her head out of reverence and to hide the tears forming in her eyes. *Thank you, Lord, for Thy abundant blessings.* She grabbed Nathan's hand under the table and gave it a quick squeeze when he finished. He looked at her curiously. She gave him a smile before turning her attention to the food.

After dining, Nathan gave Amara a tour of the residence. She was unfamiliar with the term dog trot house, so he pointed out the advantages of its design. The porch ran across the entire front of the house and the overhang provided plenty of shade on hot summer days. A breezeway split the home in two. The eastern wing of the house held the dining room, an office, parlor and a gathering room. The western portion had six bedrooms, three on each side of the hallway. Amara admired the notched wood interior walls and imagined the work Nathan and Dominic must have done piecing them together.

A brass bathtub perched in the center of the largest bedroom immediately drew Amara's attention.

"A bath?" Amara had to resist the urge to run up to the basin and throw her arms around it. She couldn't remember the last time she had a decent bath.

"There wouldn't be any chance that I could use this sometime, would there?" she asked Nathan, a beseeching note in her voice.

"If there wasn't before, there certainly is now," he replied. "How could I say no to that look?"

Amara jumped up and threw her arms around his neck.

"Thank you so much."

Peeking over his shoulder, she spotted a four-poster bed decked in a quilt with two fluffy down pillows to complete the ensemble. She disentangled herself from Nathan and ran to the bed. She smoothed the covers and ran her fingers over the crocheted edges of the pillowcase.

"Now I don't know what to do. A bath sounds lovely, but if I can lay my weary body on this feather mattress for a few hours, I think I'll have died and gone to heaven," she said with glee.

Realizing the presumption in the statement she had just uttered, Amara quickly turned back to Nathan. "Unless it's yours, of course."

"This is all yours, my dear."

A smile came to Amara's face. She turned around in a

full circle to admire everything she laid eyes on. The room had a masculine feel to it—from the large bed to the solid desk and leather wingback chairs—yet it exuded warmth and comfort.

A quick tap on the doorframe was heard and then Maria came into the room, the older men right behind her, all transporting gallons of steaming water to the room. They proceeded to fill the tub and, when it was full, everyone excused themselves, including Nathan.

Alone at last, Amara stripped the filthy clothes from her back. *If I never see these rags again, it will be one day too soon,* she thought, stealing one of her father's expressions. Using a bar of soap left by the tub, she washed her hair and then scoured every square inch of her body until her skin glowed.

That job completed, she relaxed until the water grew tepid. Reluctantly she pulled herself out of the tub, dried off with a cotton towel, and donned the nightgown laid out on top of the quilt. *It must be one of Maria's,* noted Amara, trying to pull the sleeves down closer to her wrists.

Amara crawled into bed and was asleep before her head hit the pillow.

\*\*\*

Later that night, Nathan checked in on Amara, but she was lost in slumber. He pulled up a chair and watched her for some time as she slept, a smile touching his lips as he recalled their recent weeks together.

# Chapter XXXI

Bright and early the next morning, Nathan tapped on the door and peeked in on Amara. She looked as if she hadn't moved a muscle. Quietly, he walked closer and crouched down by the side of the bed. The sun shining through the lace curtains illuminated her hair. He reached out to touch one of the locks. The short tresses were in a state of disarray, but they were laced with shades of gold and red.

"Just as lovely as when I first met you," Nathan said softly. He gently touched her cheek.

"We'll give you a few more hours, my sleeping beauty."

He soundlessly retreated from the room.

That afternoon Nathan knocked on the door and, hearing no response, pushed it open. Seeing Amara still sleeping he walked to the bedside. He stood over her, hands on hips.

***

The feeling of being observed caused Amara to groggily open her eyes.

"I was beginning to wonder about you," said Nathan.

"Why is that?" asked Amara with a perplexed look.

"You've been sleeping nearly eighteen hours."

Immediately Amara sprang up to a sitting position.

"Have I really?" She fell back and covered her face with her hands. "Everyone here must think I'm an indolent sloth."

"Nothing of the sort. They think you're exhausted. But you do need to get up sometime and face the day. Maria pressed your garments and hung them in the armoire."

Amara turned to look at the direction Nathan indicated, then her head snapped back and she looked down at what she was wearing. Her face reddened and she drew the covers up completely over her head and dropped back to the pillow.

"Can you give me a few minutes?" she asked, her voice muffled by the bedding.

"Of course," said Nathan. "Take as much time as you need." He slipped out of the room, making sure the door shut soundly behind him before he let out the laugh he had been stifling.

Amara leapt out of bed, nearly tripping on the sheets that entangled her legs. She rushed to the armoire and grabbed a dress and threw it on the bed, pulled the nightgown over her head and then pulled the dress on. A grooming kit had magically appeared on the dry sink and she tugged a hairbrush through her spiky locks and splashed water from a porcelain decanter on her face. Looking in the mirror, she reached for the pins she had noticed in the bag. Securing them, she attempted to give her hair some semblance of a style. She pinched her cheeks for color, gave her dress one last straightening, then exited the room.

\*\*\*

Supper was close to being served and all of the men sat in the gathering room discussing affairs of the ranch. Only one person from the operation was missing. No word had been heard from Dominic since he left those many months ago.

In the middle of their conversation, first one head snapped up, then the next and finally the third. Nathan's back was turned to the hallway where all the eyes were transfixed. Swinging around in his chair, he looked to see what had caught everyone's attention. He did a double take when he saw Amara hesitating by the entryway.

All the men stood and Nathan strode over to Amara and offered her his arm. He led her to the group of men, all of whom appeared to have temporarily lost their tongues.

"Evenin', Miss," someone finally said, followed by another "Evenin', Miss," and finally "Buenas noches, Señorita."

"Good evening to you, sirs," said Amara. She looked slightly uncomfortable with the attention directed towards her.

"I wasn't kidding when I said she cleaned up well, was I?" said Nathan with a chuckle.

The three other males nodded in accord.

Amara continued on. "I didn't mean to interrupt your conversation."

The men continued to stare.

"I can go see if Maria needs any help in the kitchen."

Ol' Joe was the first to find his voice again.

"No interruption a t'all, Miss."

He motioned to a chair. "You just makes yerself comfortable. Maria's got everything under control. Besides, we was just shootin' the sh...uh, breeze. Nathan here says you has an interest in seeing the rest of the property. I'd be more'n happy to give you a look-see after dinner."

"I could show you the sacred ground south of the ranch," offered Snapping Turtle.

"Maria and I show you how property ez run," offered Eduardo.

"I'm sure Amara would be happy to accompany all of you, but I reserve the honor of giving her the maiden tour of our operation myself," declared Nathan. "Assuming that is acceptable to you?" he inquired, looking to Amara for approval.

"It would only be fitting as you are the owner of this ranch," she said with a smile.

The conversation between the men resumed and, twenty minutes later, the group sat down for supper. During the meal, the men constantly talked over each other, anxious to tell stories of the trials and travails of ranch life to a new audience.

\*\*\*

Once everyone had excused themselves from the table, Nathan and Amara set off to explore the property. Wearing a borrowed poncho over her dress for warmth, Amara walked close to Nathan as they made their way around the perimeter of the cultivated fields. At one point, he grabbed her hand to help her step over the threshold of an outbuilding and didn't relinquish it as they continued along.

The act caught Amara off guard and she instinctively stiffened her arm, but relaxed when she grew accustomed to the strong grip. The night air was cool but the warmth Nathan exuded seeped into Amara's entire being.

As they continued along, Nathan pointed with pride to the structures he and Dominic had built and talked of how they broke the land and got their business up and running.

Amara expressed her amazement at how well-run their operation was, especially with the war ravaging the rest of the nation.

"It seems like the conflict is a world away from this tranquil ranch," she noted. Nathan had to agree.

They completed the excursion at the spot where they started—the front porch Nathan had described to her in vivid detail on their journey. The rocking chairs, creaky plank floorboards and the railing just the right height for Nathan to stretch his legs on looked exactly as Amara had pictured them all these weeks.

Leading her to a chair lightly rocking in the breeze, Nathan inclined his head. "Would you like to have a seat?"

"Thank you, kind sir." Amara released her hold on Nathan's hand, sat on the edge of the chair and waited for him to take the seat next to her.

When he didn't move, she looked up at him expectantly. He had a slightly odd look about him. If it had been anyone else, she would have called it nervousness but that trait was completely uncharacteristic of him.

Nathan cleared his throat. Amara waited for him to say something. But instead of speaking he dropped to one knee.

He then reached into the right hand pocket of his overcoat and pulled out a small object. Nathan gently pulled Amara's left hand towards him and proceeded to slide a gold band upon her ring finger. Amara's free hand flew to her mouth.

"Amara?"

"Y-Yes," she stammered.

"Last month we were married by Father O'Reilly in the presence of God. You may have had your doubts about the legitimacy of our marriage, but I never did. When I vowed to be your husband until death do us part, I meant it. I want our marriage to be a true one."

Biting her lip to stem the tears, Amara took in a choppy breath and tried to quell her sniffling.

"Nathan, I want that too."

His gray eyes lit up. "I love you, Amara," he said, looking deep into her eyes. "And I hope someday you can grow to love me."

"Grow to love you? You have no idea, Nathan." Her voice rose with emotion as she gently put her hand on his cheek.

"I asked you to be honest with me and now I'm going to be honest with you," said Amara shakily. "This may sound terribly shallow, but I was infatuated the first time I laid eyes on you. You were the most handsome man I'd ever seen, and I knew you were a good person regardless of what you were trying to lead me to believe."

They both smiled at that recollection. Amara lowered her hand and paused for a moment as a darker memory surfaced. "My heart nearly shattered when I thought you'd been untrue to me."

A pained look crossed Nathan's face. "I'm so sorry, Amara."

"There's nothing to apologize for, Nathan. Everything happened as it needed to for us to be together." She smiled at him again.

"Each experience we've shared over the last few months has revealed more of your inner character to me," said Amara with certainty. "That infatuation I had for you became something deeper. Once I recognized my feelings for what they really were, I thought my heart would burst if I couldn't express my true sentiments to you." Amara placed her hands on top of Nathan's outstretched palms. "I love you too, Nathan, and I will love you for the rest of my life."

Nathan gently squeezed her hands. "Then will you accept this ring and vow to be my lawfully wedded wife, through sickness and health, through richer and poorer..."

"Through anything," said Amara, throwing her arms around Nathan's neck.

This time Amara received a kiss that was more befitting a new bride. Nathan tilted her head back with his hand and his lips devoured hers. She felt as if she were flying over the earth like the eagle they had observed on the trail.

When they released from their embrace, Nathan stood up and swept his arm under Amara's legs. He carried her to the entrance of the house, kicked open the door, and they crossed the threshold to begin their new life together.

# EPILOGUE

It was a perfect late spring evening and the sounds of birds calling, and a light breeze whispering through the treetops added to the ambiance. No matter how many times Amara took in the view from their front porch, she could never get over the beauty of the land on which they had the privilege of living. Her heart swelled with pride as she looked at the herds, and the plains dotted with bluebonnets that seemed to stretch out forever. She was especially pleased as she envisioned where the hospital and school would stand one day. The church was already beginning to take form on the far edge of the land.

Nathan sat by her side, leaning back in his chair with his legs stretched out in front of him. Instinctively he grabbed Amara's hand as if he knew what she was thinking. She cupped her right hand over their intertwined fingers. *I still cannot believe how blessed I am,* she thought, her face beaming. *Even in my most vivid dreams, I never imagined such a wonderful existence.* In one year's time, her life had drastically changed. She may have questioned the direction she was being led at times, but she knew God had a plan for her life. *For our lives,* she thought contentedly.

Reaching over, Nathan patted her growing belly with his left hand. "Hello, little one."

Amara put her hand on her abdomen as the movement she felt earlier grew more insistent. "He's a spirited tyke, just like his Uncle James. We may regret naming the baby after him."

"What makes you so certain it's a boy?" asked Nathan. "My mother will be displeased if we've been calling her namesake James all these months instead of Josephine. I can just picture her now, standing on a cloud, hands held in a saintly fashion, shaking her head at our foolishness."

The image made Amara laugh.

"Sorry, Mother Simmons, we'll name our next child after you. This little fellow has to be a boy. They don't allow girls to be priests."

"I guess I can't argue that logic," replied Nathan, planting a kiss on the palm of Amara's hand.

Checkers lay between them as he routinely did, always on the lookout for a stray rabbit or squirrel foolish enough to enter his domain. Sure enough, his ears pricked up and he was off like a shot over the ridge.

The couple looked in the direction he had gone, expecting him to reappear shortly. A few minutes later, they did spot something but it wasn't the dog. Two men came to view as they crested the rise. The animal trailed behind them.

"That's odd," said Nathan. "Checkers isn't normally that friendly with strangers. Stay here, Amara. I'll go see what they want."

He stepped off the porch and strode towards the men, both of whom wore ragged military uniforms. Amara squinted, trying to make out their figures. *If my eyes aren't deceiving me, it looks as one is wearing gray and one is clad in blue,* she thought with confusion. The war was over, but she had always assumed it would take years before the hard feelings between the North and South were set aside.

Amara was startled to see Nathan break into a run and charge up to the men. He tackled the one wearing blue. *What in the Lord's name is he doing?*

She picked up her skirts and trotted towards the trio as quickly as she could with her expanded girth. Amara was dismayed to see the two men wrestling on the ground. At least no blows were being thrown, but what on earth had gotten into her husband?

"Nathan Michael Edward Simmons, what in the name of the Lord are you doing?" Amara panted out as she reached him. She grabbed hold of the back of his collar. "That is no way to greet a guest."

The two men stopped in mid roll and both fell to their backs, trying to catch their breath while they laughed uproariously.

"This isn't a visitor," exclaimed Nathan, punching the man in the shoulder. "It's Dominic, come back from the dead."

The men stood up and dusted themselves off, still chortling. Remembering his manners, Dominic wiped his hand on his sleeve and formally offered it to Amara.

"It's a pleasure to meet you, Ma'am." She automatically took his hand and looked at him incredulously.

"Dominic?" She threw her arms around him. "The Lord be praised."

Wiping tears from her eyes, she loosened her grip on him and turned to greet the other soldier.

She froze midstride.

"Oh my God." She inched forward hesitantly. "Can it possibly be you?"

"It is me, Sis." The man reached out to embrace her.

"What are you doing here, Michael?" she asked in amazement as she pulled back to look at him. "How in the world did you ever find me?"

"It took some work but Father O'Reilly set me off in the right direction. Along the way I encountered this fellow who, coincidentally enough, was headed the same way."

Nathan watched the exchange between the two.

Amara held onto her brother's hands as if he were going to disappear if she let go. She couldn't stop shaking her head in wonder. She finally let go of one of his hands when Nathan stepped up to greet the man.

"I'm Nathan Simmons, Amara's husband," he said, extending his hand.

Michael shook his hand and they sized each other up.

Nathan furrowed his brow as he looked closer at the man. "Have we met? I have this uncanny feeling I've seen you somewhere before."

Michael scrutinized him. "You do have a striking resemblance to a Union soldier I encountered in a skirmish once. Strangest story, I had taken a bullet to the leg..."

"And the enemy officer patched you up," interrupted Nathan.

"Yes, as a matter of fact, that is the short version of the story. How did you come to have knowledge of this?" asked Michael with a note of surprise.

"I knew I recognized those blue eyes. They're an exact match to my wife's. You're the man I gave my belt to on the battlefield."

A look of revelation crossed Michael's face. "You're the soldier who saved my life?" He took a step backwards in astonishment. "I always prayed I would be able to thank that man in person some day."

Amara could hardly believe her ears. "One miracle after another," she exclaimed. "For both of you to not only survive the war but end up on our doorstep on the same day..." She looked over the three men and her joy had no bounds.

"What have I done to deserve this, Lord?" she questioned out loud, looking at the skies above her.

"Everything," said Nathan, wrapping her in his arms. "Everything."

# Acknowledgements

For my husband John Lauer, our children Stephanie, Nicholas, Samantha and Elizabeth, and all my family and friends for supporting and encouraging me in my endeavors throughout the years.

For William (Doc) and Donna Syverson, who introduced me to their ancestor Ira, whose real life Civil War experiences inspired this book, and for sharing with me their vast knowledge of Civil War history to ensure the accuracy of this novel.

For Melissa Westemeier, my writing partner, for holding me accountable to my commitment to produce one new chapter of this book every month for more than two years, and for using her writing, teaching and editing skills to help me transition from a journalist to a novelist.

For the numerous people who read this manuscript in its various stages. The book was enriched by your honest feedback.

For Anna Coltran, of Belle Gente Photography in Atlanta, who took the beautiful photos for the front and back covers of this book.

For my publisher, Ellen Gable Hrkach, and everyone at Full Quiver Publishing, for having faith in me and my writing ability, and helping bring my dream and this story to life.

To Ira Simmons, for his service as a soldier in the U.S. Army during the Civil War. Although he made the ultimate sacrifice for his country, his spirit lives on in these words.

# Father Thomas O'Reilly - biography

Father Thomas O'Reilly was pastor of Immaculate Conception Church in Atlanta, Georgia during the Civil War. O'Reilly used his church as a hospital for both Federal and Confederate soldiers. When Major General William T. Sherman's army reached the gates of the city in July 1864, Fr. O'Reilly went to the battlefields, ministering to the wounded, saying Mass in the field and performing Last Rites. In November 1864, he learned of Sherman's plan to burn Atlanta, including several churches of different denominations. Father O'Reilly approached Major General Henry Slocum, an acquaintance and member of Sherman's staff and argued that burning the churches would be an affront to heaven. He warned that he would use his influence with the many Irish troops to foment mutiny if the churches were destroyed and he used the threat of excommunication against any Catholic soldier who participated in the burning. Sherman eventually agreed to spare the houses of worship. Placing guards at the churches and the courthouse, Sherman even ordered buildings in the immediate vicinity not be burned to control the flames. Nearly 400 houses were spared. The spared churches were used by returning Atlanta residents as places of refuge. In 1869, the old Immaculate Conception Church was moved a block away, and a new church, the Shrine of the Immaculate Conception, was constructed in its place. Father O'Reilly died in 1872 and is buried in the basement of his beloved church. A monument to him is located on the grounds of the current Atlanta City Hall.

Source: "The Civil War in Georgia – Commemorating 150 Years" (www.gacivilwar.org)

## About the Author

An avid reader and history buff since childhood, Amanda Lauer fulfilled a lifelong goal with the publication of her debut novel, *A World Such as Heaven Intended*. Lauer learned the technical aspects of writing as a proofreader in the insurance, newspaper and collegiate arenas. Over the last ten years, she has had more than twelve hundred articles published in newspapers and magazines throughout the United States.

Lauer is the co-author of *Celebrate Appleton, A 150th Birthday Photo Album*, and contributed to the books *Expressions of ITP...Inside Stories* and *Living Virtuously: Keeping Your Heart & Home*. In addition to her writing career, Lauer is involved in the health and wellness industry, striving to spread the message of true health — physical, mental and financial.

Residents of northeast Wisconsin, Lauer and her husband John have been married thirty-three years. They are involved in their church and community and in their spare time travel for business and pleasure, play golf, run, bike, read, and further their education in the area of personal development. They are the proud parents of four young adult children, have a son-in-law and daughter-in-law, and are grandparents to one grandson.

Author's website:
http://aworldsuchasheavenintended.wordpress.com


For more FQ Publishing books, please check out our website:

www.fullquiverpublishing.com

Made in the USA
Coppell, TX
07 June 2024

33237050R00134